"So you're Scott Harris's brother,"

Hank said, more as a fact than a question. "How long do you plan on staying in Crystal Creek?"

"I'm not sure. I got no real reason to stay." Jeff shook his head to clear the picture of Beverly Townsend that suddenly popped into his head. "Of course, I got no real reason to leave yet, either."

"I hear you're an oilman. Are you one of those fancy geologist fellas who make their decisions on facts and figures?"

"I guess I'm more of a traditional wildcatter," Jeff answered. "Sure, I look at maps and statistics, but what I go by is my gut feeling. It's like there's a vibration leading me to the oil. No one else can feel it, so they think I'm nuts. But I know when there's oil under the ground as soon as I step on it."

"Hot dang! You *are* an oilman." Hank nodded, and his thin lips spread into a wide grin. "I've got me this piece of land down on the gulf coast…"

Special thanks and acknowledgment to Kathy Clark
for her contribution to the Crystal Creek series.

Special thanks and acknowledgment to Sutton Press Inc.
for its contribution to the concept for the Crystal Creek series.

Published September 1993

ISBN-13: 978-0-373-25086-8
ISBN-10:   0-373-25086-X

HEARTS AGAINST THE WIND

Hearts Against the Wind

KATHY CLARK

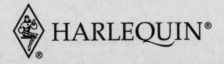

HARLEQUIN®

TORONTO • NEW YORK • LONDON
AMSTERDAM • PARIS • SYDNEY • HAMBURG
STOCKHOLM • ATHENS • TOKYO • MILAN • MADRID
PRAGUE • WARSAW • BUDAPEST • AUCKLAND

DEEP IN THE HEART
Barbara Kaye

COWBOYS AND CABERNET
Margot Dalton

AMARILLO BY MORNING
Bethany Campbell

WHITE LIGHTNING
Sharon Brondos

EVEN THE NIGHTS ARE BETTER
Margot Dalton

AFTER THE LIGHTS GO OUT
Barbara Kaye

HEARTS AGAINST THE WIND
Kathy Clark

THE THUNDER ROLLS
Bethany Campbell

GUITARS, CADILLACS
Cara West

STAND BY YOUR MAN
Kathy Clark

NEW WAY TO FLY
Margot Dalton

EVERYBODY'S TALKIN'
Barbara Kaye

Dear Reader,

Welcome back to Crystal Creek! In the heart of Texas Hill Country, the McKinneys have been ranching, living and loving for generations, but the future promises changes none of these good folks could ever imagine!

Crystal Creek itself is the product of many imaginations, but the stories began to take shape when some of your favorite authors—Barbara Kaye, Margot Dalton, Bethany Campbell, Cara West, Kathy Clark and Sharon Brondos—all got together with me just outside of Austin to explore the Hill Country, and to dream up the kinds of romances such a setting would provide. For several days, we roamed the countryside, where generous Texans opened their historic homes to us, and gave us insights into their lives. We ate barbecue, we visited an ostrich farm and we mapped out our plans to give you the linked stories you love, with a true Texas flavor and all the elements you've come to expect in your romance reading: compelling, contemporary characters caught in conflicts that reflect today's dilemmas.

Old Hank takes a shine to Scott Harris's irredeemable brother Jeff in Kathy Clark's *Hearts Against the Wind*. He senses a true oilman beneath that happy-go-lucky charm and those drop-dead good looks. And Beverly Townsend, who's been looking so hard for the perfect romance, is quite startled when it sneaks up behind her from the unlikeliest and most unsuitable quarter imaginable!

Next month, Ken Slattery, a man of few words, decides what he wants and goes after it with an admirable single-mindedness. But the lady the Double C's foreman has set his sights on has eyes for only one man—her eight-year-old son. Add to the brew a moody sense of impending violence, an unpredictable and emotionally unstable ex-husband, and a heart-thumping climax, and you won't want to miss Bethany Campbell's *The Thunder Rolls*.

C'mon down to Crystal Creek—home of sultry Texas drawls, smooth Texas charm and tall, sexy Texans!

Marsha Zinberg
Executive Editor
Crystal Creek

A Note from the Author

I was born and raised in Texas, so the Crystal Creek series has a special meaning for me. Handsome cowboys, beauty queens, oilmen, cattle barons and plain ol'country folk are more than fiction...they're Texas traditions.

I now live in Colorado with my family, but my roots will always be in Texas. I hope, through the wonderful stories of the residents of Crystal Creek, you'll fall in love with the beauty and majesty of that great state, too.

Kathy Clark

Cast of Characters
AT THE DOUBLE C RANCH

John Travis (J.T.) McKinney	Rancher, owner of the Double C, his family's ranch. A man who knows his own mind.
Cynthia Page McKinney	J.T.'s wife. An ex-Bostonian bank executive learning to do things the Texas way.
Tyler McKinney	J.T.'s eldest son, a graduate of Rice University. Now he wants to grow grapes in his daddy's pasture.
Cal McKinney	J.T.'s second son, an irresistible and irrepressible rodeo cowboy.
Serena Davis	The boot maker who's turned Cal's head.
Lynn McKinney	J.T.'s only daughter. She bucks the trend by raising Thoroughbreds in quarter-horse country.
Hank Travis	J.T.'s ancient grandfather. Old Hank has seen and done it all.
Ruth Holden	Californian vintner, daughter of Dan Holden, J.T.'s old army buddy. Ruth is visiting the Double C to help Tyler plan his vineyard.

AT THE CIRCLE T RANCH

Carolyn Randolph Townsend	J.T.'s sister-in-law and neighbor.
Beverly Townsend	Carolyn's daughter and a former Miss Texas.
Vernon Trent	Real-estate agent, and childhood friend of Carolyn's.

AT THE LONGHORN

Dottie Jones	Owner of the Longhorn Motel and Coffee Shop.
Nora Jones	Dottie's son's ex-wife.

AT THE HOLE IN THE WALL

Scott Harris   He's exchanged his pinstripes for chaps and a
                      Stetson, to create his dream, the Hole in the Wall
                      Dude Ranch.

Valerie Drayton   Scott's new wife and partner in the ranch.

Jeff Harris   Scott's brother. Once the Hole in the Wall puts a
                      few bucks in his pocket, he's heading for his true
                      love: the Texas oil fields.

CHAPTER ONE

"THERE JUST AREN'T any good men left."
Beverly Townsend leaned against the solid
oak bar inside the lounge at the Hole in the
Wall Dude Ranch. Her gaze followed the
bride and groom as they swirled among the
other dancers on the dance floor.

"Yeah, I agree," Jeff Harris said, then as
Beverly cast him an amused look, he hur-
riedly revised, "I mean there aren't any good
women left either." His attention returned to
the newlyweds who, wrapped in each other's
embrace, were oblivious to the crowd around
them.

For several minutes Jeff and Beverly stood
silent, weighed down by their thoughts—
thoughts that were running on a parallel
course. The groom, who happened to be
Jeff's brother, and his smiling bride contin-

ued to move around the floor, dancing slowly in the intimate circle of each other's arms.

Beverly sighed as they passed directly in front of her. Scott, the groom, was handsome, intelligent, wealthy—he owned the Hole in the Wall. He could have been her Mr. Right. Why, then, had fate chosen that same time to drop Valerie Drayton—now Valerie Harris—into his life and into his arms?

If Val hadn't entered the picture, Beverly was certain she and Scott could have made a terrific couple. If only they'd had a little more time together, Beverly was sure he would have fallen in love with her. If only…

But, as disappointed as she was, Beverly couldn't dislike Val. It was easy to see what Scott saw in her and why he had, just an hour earlier, made her his wife. Val was pretty, in an outdoorsy sort of way, and she could hold her own with anyone around the ranch. In fact, it was mostly due to her energy and expertise that the Hole in the Wall had become such a successful guest ranch so quickly.

When Scott had first hired her to coordinate the building and day-to-day operations of the twenty-five-hundred-acre resort, the people around Crystal Creek had watched skeptically.

Actually, the locals were more concerned because Scott, an outsider, had come along, bought the land and built, of all things, a dude ranch, complete with gift shops, restaurant, tennis courts and swimming pool. And something that had caused Beverly's mother particular anxiety—an exotic game preserve. But Carolyn Townsend and the other locals had accepted Valerie, who had been working on ranches since she was a teenager and who fit into the rural routine with ease. And through her, the townsfolk had gradually warmed to Scott, whose sophisticated reserve had taken more time to adjust to the casual life-style of the Texas Hill Country.

Everyone had encouraged the romance between the ranch manager and her handsome boss.

"Do you want to dance?"

Beverly jumped and turned to Jeff. She'd completely forgotten he was standing beside her.

"No thanks. I'm not in the mood." She didn't try to hide her melancholy. Of all the

people in the room, Jeff would best understand how she felt at the moment. After all,
he'd been interested in Val until Scott staked
his claim.

"But it's a tradition that the best man
dances with the maid of honor." Jeff gave
her a wolfish grin and adjusted the silver
clasp of his bolo tie with exaggerated care.
"It's not often you're going to see me
dressed up like this. I'm more of a jeans and
T-shirt kind of guy." His bold gaze drifted
down Beverly's ruffled rose cowgirl blouse
and calf-length denim skirt that had followed
the theme of a country wedding. "Although
I suspect you're used to getting all dolled up
for parties and things," he added, an unexpected hint of disapproval shading his voice.

Beverly studied the man next to her. She
still found it difficult to believe that Jeff was
Scott's brother. They were as different as
night and day, not just in looks, but in tem-
perament and attitude. Scott, with his ash-
blond hair and gray eyes, was tall and gorgeous, besides being as steady and reliable
as the huge, ancient oak trees that grew on
the ranch.

Jeff, on the other hand, could only be counted on to be unpredictable. A little taller than his brother, Jeff was certainly no less handsome than Scott. Beverly could easily picture him in the role of a rogue with his dark brown hair, a little too long in the back and always falling across his forehead, and his mischievous blue-gray eyes. In fact, Beverly had noticed a good percentage of the female population of Crystal Creek drooling over the younger Harris brother. And Jeff, in turn, was living up to his reputation by charming every woman between the age of puberty and death.

If she could believe the gossip, which was the lifeblood in a small town like Crystal Creek, he'd almost killed a man in a bar fight and he'd left behind a string of broken hearts without the least sign of remorse. He'd blown into town about a month ago and no one knew when he would disappear again, riding off into the sunset in search of adventure. Jeff, it seemed, was as determined to remain footloose and fancy-free as Scott was to put down strong, deep roots.

If only Scott had fallen in love with Beverly. But, with the crumbled remains of a partially eaten wedding cake serving as a depressing reminder, it was too late.

"I think I've had enough *fun* for one evening," she stated, placing her half-empty glass on the bar. "I'm going to give my regards to the happy couple, then go home and cry myself to sleep."

A slow, sexy smile stretched across Jeff's face. "Beverly Townsend crying over a man? Ah, come on, darlin'. I can't believe that."

"I'll bet there's a tear or two inside you right now for ol' Val, even if you won't let it out."

"Don't be silly. Val's just a friend," he said with a casual shrug.

But Beverly caught a glimpse of regret as Jeff's gaze involuntarily moved to his brother's new wife. Somehow it made her feel better to know someone was sharing her pain, however selfish that might be.

"How long will you be staying in Crystal Creek?" she asked.

"I haven't made any plans."

"I heard long-range planning wasn't one of your strong points."

"Long-range, short-range—I'm just not a planning kind of guy. I like to listen to the wind as it whispers the names of places I've never been, things I've never done and people I've never met." He leveled a measuring look at her. "You had your chance. You could have made a clean break from this town. Why did you come back?"

Beverly blinked, caught off guard by his sudden seriousness. "Because all my friends and family are here," she answered with only a slight hesitation.

"That's a crock..." he exclaimed. "You came back because you didn't have the guts to break away from the security of your little cocoon. Crystal Creek isn't the real world, you know. There's excitement, endless possibilities and new horizons out there. You won't drop off the edge of the earth if you go past the city limits sign."

"You don't know what you're talking about." Beverly bristled, straightening and meeting his eyes with a disdainful glare. "I *chose* to come back here because there were people who loved me and were waiting to welcome me home. But you wouldn't understand about that, would you?''

A frown twitched across his dark eyebrows, then quickly disappeared. ''I like to keep things simple. No roots, no regrets...''

''And no responsibilities,'' Beverly added.

''Yeah, sort of like you, huh?''

''Don't try to turn this around. I'm not afraid to take on responsibility.''

''Such as?''

She opened her mouth to give him a hot retort, but couldn't think of an honest reply. Even though she was twenty-five years old with a master's degree from the University of Texas, she still lived at home with her mother. Volunteering at the hospital at least two afternoons a week and taking on an occasional modeling job didn't exactly qualify her as the responsibility poster girl.

Still, Jeff was the last person who had the right to accuse her. ''You wouldn't know responsibility if it bit you on the...''

''No, but at least I'm honest with myself.'' One corner of his lips curved up in a grin that seemed to imply he knew a lot more about her than she thought. "And I'm not afraid to push the boundaries to see how far I can go. I let my intuition guide me, stopping me in one place for a while, then telling me when it's time to leave."

"Yeah, you already told me—you listen to the wind." Beverly gave a scornful laugh. "Well, you should listen to it saying that it's time you grew up!"

He flashed her that killer grin. "Why should I? I enjoy my freedom." He paused a few seconds, then added, "Envious?"

"Of course not!" she retorted, but deep inside, she knew he'd touched a raw nerve. She *wasn't* living the life she wanted to live. Not that she wanted to travel from town to town, never putting down stakes. She just wanted to find her own place in the world.

"You should give it a try. Do something just because you *want* to and not because it might somehow affect your career or your future. Listen to that Texas wind. It's more eloquent than the wind in any other part of the world. It's filled with tall tales and sad stories. It carries the voices of men and women who were brave enough to break away from their secure, predictable lives and strike out for something better. It's out there, Beverly. All you have to do is listen.''

Beverly could scarcely contain her anger. How dared this man, who made a joke out of everything, presume to tell her what to do? ''If I want your advice about my life, I'll ask for it. You just arrived here a few weeks ago. You don't know anything about anyone. Least of all me.''

''Can't we leave the two of you alone for five minutes without you coming to blows?''

Beverly whirled around. She'd been so caught up in her argument with Jeff that she hadn't noticed Scott and Val's approach. ''We...uh, I was on my way over to congratulate you two and wish you a lifetime of happiness,'' she managed to say, her usual poise shaken. ''And to tell you that I've got to leave.''

''You're leaving so soon? But the party's just getting under way,'' Val said. She looked genuinely disappointed.

''I've got a splitting headache. Must be some sort of allergy,'' Beverly responded. At least the headache part was true, but it had nothing to do with the pollen count.

Beside her, Jeff snorted and Beverly tossed him a warning glare.

Beverly gave Valerie a hug, then hesitated a split second before giving Scott a clumsy embrace. God, she wanted to get home, away from all this happiness and love. "Thanks for asking me to be your maid of honor, Valerie."

"Thanks for accepting. It meant a lot to both of us," Valerie said, unconsciously snuggling closer to Scott as he slipped his arm around her waist. "I realize we planned this wedding pretty quickly, but once Scott and I decided to get married, we didn't see any sense in waiting."

"Besides, tourist season will soon be at a peak, so this was the last chance we'd have until fall," Scott added, giving his bride an affectionate look. "I didn't want Val to stay in that guest cabin a minute longer than necessary."

Valerie smiled at her husband, then turned back to Jeff. "Oh, by the way, you can move into the cabin as soon as I get the rest of my things moved to Scott's next week.''

''Thanks.'' Jeff accepted the offer, but hurried to add, ''But I shouldn't be needing it long. I plan on being on my way in a couple of weeks.''

Beverly couldn't take any more of the cheerful chitchat. ''I've really got to go... good night.'' She brushed past them and hurried toward the door, anxious to get away before she embarrassed herself in front of everyone. But luck was not with her as her cousin, Lynn McKinney, stepped into Beverly's path.

''Doesn't Val look beautiful? And that cake! I haven't seen anything that big since Dad's wedding to Cynthia. And isn't Val's mother sweet? To think, they hadn't seen each other in all those years, but now they're close again....'' Lynn's chatter stopped abruptly as she peered more closely at Beverly. ''What's wrong, Bev? Are you sick?''

''Just a headache,'' Beverly answered, trying to force a smile.

''Well, go home and take a couple aspirins or something. Sam and I will pick you up in the morning at nine,'' Lynn continued, still watching her friend carefully. ''Is that too early?''

''What?''

''We're going to the lake house tomorrow, remember? Now don't tell me you forgot about it! This is the first weekend we've been able to plan something together in weeks.''

Beverly noticed Lynn's brothers, Tyler and Cal, approaching with their respective fiancés, and she became more desperate than ever to escape. ''Yeah, sure. Nine o'clock's fine. See you then.''

It wasn't until she was in the parking lot, sitting safely in the solitude of her new white sports car that Beverly realized she'd committed herself to going. While Scott and Val were spending their honeymoon in the Bahamas, Beverly would be suffering through a whole day of watching Lynn and her fiancé, Sam Russell, share sweet, private glances.

It seemed like the love bug was biting everyone in Crystal Creek...everyone but Beverly. She gave a mirthless heart-wrenching chuckle. They all thought she had her pick of men. Wouldn't they be surprised to find out she'd *never* been in love!

It might have been a different story with Scott. Oh, she'd known what she felt for him wasn't real love. But the attraction had been there. Maybe it could have developed into genuine affection over time.

She'd known she and Scott were not really suited to each other. Scott liked quiet evenings at home. His idea of a good time was to throw a steak on the barbecue, open a bottle of wine, perhaps put on some classical music and enjoy the company of whomever he was with. Beverly, on the other hand, was the original party gal. She loved noise, excitement, crowds and dancing. How many times had she been irritated with Scott for refusing to go out?

So why had she felt so sad at his wedding? She was Beverly Townsend—used to men falling at her feet. She knew she was beautiful. It would have been stupid to deny it or pretend not to know it. Her beauty was completely natural. When she was a child, people would stop her mother in stores and comment on Beverly's perfect features. Her father had taken her everywhere with him, bragging about how pretty she was and getting her to show off her equestrian skills.

Beverly had always enjoyed the attention. But most of all she'd enjoyed knowing how proud her father was of her. She'd always been Daddy's little girl. His death a couple of years ago had been a crushing blow. But the pattern had been set. She knew what to do to make people notice her.

But, with the years, had come the realization that no one seemed able to see beyond her huge, deep blue eyes or flawless complexion. No one tried to see if there was anything of value beneath that perfection.

Whether it was because she didn't think she would be able to change their minds or whether she didn't want to make the effort, Beverly had accepted their attitudes. She knew her beauty was God given. She certainly hadn't done anything other than use it to her best advantage. Getting by on her looks became a habit. It made her popular. It helped her get better grades. It was her security blanket.

She brushed away the tears that were

threatening to spill, and turned the key in the ignition. She had to get home.

The ranch house at the Circle T was quiet when she arrived. Her mother was still at the wedding and the staff were probably already asleep. After parking her car under the carport, Beverly walked around to the back of the house where she had a private entrance to her bedroom through a French door. Centered in a flagstone patio and surrounded by a rock garden, the oval swimming pool sparkled in the moonlight like a polished opal.

Deciding a few laps might clear her head, Beverly quickly changed into her swimsuit and poised on the end of the diving board. A full June moon dominated the velvet sky and danced on the surface of the pool as if teasing her with its shimmering double image.

I'm nearly thirty, Beverly thought. *And what have I accomplished?* Beverly knew that, figuratively, she was poised on the edge of the rest of her life. Oh sure, she had her beauty contest trophies. From the first one she'd won as the rodeo queen when she was a freshman at Crystal Creek High, to the assorted beauty awards she'd collected while in college, then through her progression from Miss Austin to Miss Texas to the Miss America contest, Beverly had used her looks to get her whatever she wanted. That included two full scholarships to college, a constantly expanding wardrobe, money in the bank and her car. But when she'd finished as first runner-up in the Miss America contest, Beverly had suddenly realized there were no more rungs to climb on the beauty-queen ladder.

And now, two years later, Beverly was no closer to finding a satisfactory career than she had been in high school. And she was certainly no closer to a meaningful relationship with a man. But then, how could she hope to find a man who would love her for the woman inside when even she didn't know who that woman was?

With a lithe jump, she pushed herself upward, arched and shattered the moon's reflection into a million ripples. The water, still holding the heat of the day, curled around her, sensuous in its intimacy. Beverly's arms reached out in rhythmic strokes, pulling her to the opposite end of the pool. She touched the concrete wall and immediately turned and began another lap. If the soothing liquid didn't ease the strain from her, at least the exercise would help her get to sleep.

THE MUSIC from the country and western band spilled out the door as Jeff opened it and walked outside. As the door swung shut behind him, the party noise was muffled, replaced by the nighttime sounds of the ranch.

Horses shifted, stomping the ground and nickering as they settled for the evening. Soft bellows of cows and the answering cries of their calves traveled through the still night air from the pasture.

Jeff's boots clattered against the wooden boards as he walked along the porch that ran all the way around the lodge. An owl hooted from the branch of a nearby live oak tree.

A lonely cloud drifted across the full moon, shrouding the yard in darkness. When a match scraped across the rough cedar rail and flared into a tiny blaze, the owl spread its wings and disappeared into the darkness. Jeff jumped, startled to discover he wasn't alone.

"All the excitement's inside," a voice commented.

Jeff peered into the gloom, but it wasn't until the cloud freed the moonlight that he was able to make out the figure of an old man sitting on the porch swing.

"Thanks, but I've had enough excitement for one night," Jeff replied. "Do you mind if I join you?"

The old man shrugged. "Suit yourself."

Jeff sat on the wide top rail, one leg resting on the rail and the other braced against the porch. He leaned back against a rugged wooden post. For several minutes he sat quietly, watching out of the corner of his eyes as the old man smoked a hand-rolled cigarette.

"You're Hank, Lynn and Tyler's grandfather, aren't you?" Jeff asked.

"*Great*-grandfather."

Jeff had heard a lot about Hank Travis. He was a living legend in Crystal Creek. His ninety-nine years had spanned decades of change in the world. And his mind was sharp enough to remember it all from the time he was old enough to take note of current events.

But what interested Jeff was Hank's history in oil exploration. He'd been a very successful oilman in his prime.

"And you're Scott Harris's brother," Hank stated, more as a fact than a question. "How long you plan on stayin' in Crystal Creek?"

"I'm not sure. Maybe tomorrow…maybe after my birthday in a few weeks. I've got no real reason to stay. But I don't have a reason to leave yet, either."

"I heard you're an oilman," Hank said, apparently reading Jeff's thoughts.

"I like to think so," Jeff answered, and one corner of his mouth lifted into a self-deprecating grin. "But next to you, I'm a rank amateur."

"Hell, don't knock experience. Every minute a feller spends on a site, he learns somethin'. Why, I remember ridin' up to take my daddy his lunch and seein' the top blow off the Spindletop well. Yep, only seven years old I was then, but I remember it clear as day. That black gold just come gushin' outta there like a fountain. Wasn't but a few minutes till we were all covered from head to toe in oil." Hank chuckled. "Shoot, I'll never forget the lickin' my mama gave me when I got home. But I was hooked. From that day on, I knew I didn't have blood runnin' through my veins—I had oil.''

"Yeah, I know what you mean," Jeff agreed. "Ever since the bottom dropped out of the oil industry, I've been trying to think of some other line of work to get into. But there's just nothing like the anticipation of the search or the excitement of the drilling. It's like a treasure hunt. The clues are all there. All a person has to do is read them correctly, then choose the right spot to sink the casings.''

Hank leveled his steady gaze at Jeff. Even though they were shielded by the thick lenses of wire-rimmed glasses, Hank's eyes were not those of an elderly man. They were keen and observant, and Jeff felt as if he'd been weighed, measured and thoroughly evaluated by the time Hank managed a companionable smile that barely disturbed his tanned, creased cheeks.

"I'm tired of all this noise," Hank said, pushing himself to his feet. "You got a car?''

"Uh...yes," Jeff answered. "Actually, it's a truck."

"Even better." Hank nodded. "Gimme a good ol' pickup any day. Let's go. You can take me home now."

Jeff stifled a smile at the old man's imperious attitude. He noticed that even though Hank used a cane to walk, his movements were surprisingly spry for a person of his age.

"I don't get off the ranch much anymore," Hank continued.

"Why not?"

"Well, for one thing I banged up my hip in an oil well blowout—must be close to forty years ago now—and then I broke the same hip twenty-five years later."

"You look like you get around pretty well to me."

"Some days are better than others. It weren't so bad when I still could get around in my pickup. But they said I was too old to drive. Can you imagine that? Take away a man's keys and you take away his freedom. Hell, I don't feel any older than I did when I was in my sixties." He held on to the railing, waving off Jeff's offer of a helping hand. "It's hell gettin' old. How old are you, boy?"

"I'll be thirty in a couple weeks."

"Thirty. Ahh…to be thirty again. I was in my prime."

"Yeah, well, I feel like I'm all washed up," Jeff commented. He and Hank walked slowly across the manicured lawn that bordered the pathways from the main lodge to the guest cabins and the parking lot.

"Havin' some tough luck?"

"You could say that." Jeff sighed. Actually, that was an understatement. Out of his past six jobs, he'd come up with four dry holes. That was less than a fifty percent average. And that was why he was killing time at his brother's ranch, waiting for a job offer or even a hint of a job that would take him back on the road. "My methods are a little unorthodox in today's scientific society."

"So you're not one of those geologist fellas that makes your decisions on facts and figures?"

Jeff gave Hank a curious look. It was a casual question, but something in Hank's attitude told Jeff it was a more complex inquiry than it appeared. He hesitated a moment, because his approach was unconventional, and some people didn't understand. But Jeff could feel a kinship with the old man.

"I guess you could say I'm more of a traditional wildcatter," Jeff said. "I look at the maps and study the statistics. But what I really go by is my gut feeling. It's like there's a vibration leading me to the oil. No one else can feel it, so they think I'm nuts. But I *know* whether or not there's oil under the ground as soon as I step on it."

Hank stopped walking with a suddenness that made Jeff look at him with concern. But instead of pain on the old man's features, Jeff saw unmasked delight.

"Hot dang. You *are* an oilman." Hank nodded and his thin lips spread into a wide grin. "I've got this piece of land down near the Gulf Coast...."

CHAPTER TWO

"IT LOOKS LIKE perfect weather today," Lynn commented as Sam drove her and Beverly out of Crystal Creek toward Lake Travis.

Thoughts of the weather were the farthest thing from Beverly's mind. She still couldn't believe she'd let Lynn talk her into tagging along. How much fun could it be to spend all day on a relatively small powerboat with a couple who were wildly in love? In her current mood, being the odd one out would only accentuate her loneliness.

The car stopped in the driveway next to the lake house that was jointly owned by the McKinney and Townsend families. Actually, the land had been inherited by Carolyn and her sister Pauline, Lynn's mother, from their father. They'd decided to turn it into a family retreat and had had the large, airy house built when their children were very young so they would always have a place to go for family gatherings away from the constant demands of their ranches.

Beverly climbed out of the car and stretched. She was still tired. Even after what must have been thirty laps of the pool, she'd taken ages to fall asleep last night. She suspected that as soon as she sprawled out on the cushions of the open bow with the sun beating down on her, she would doze off.

Already, the air was hot and heavy with humidity. The hum of cicadas vibrated from the oak trees, and dozens of birds flitted from their nests to the ground as they searched for food to feed their fledglings.

Beverly felt the reluctance to enjoy the day ease out of her. This had always been one of her favorite places. There was a peace and calm here that she never felt at the ranch.

"Remember when we were kids and would come here for the weekends?" Lynn asked, apparently sharing Beverly's thoughts. "We would take Grandma's quilts out on the porch and make a giant pallet."

"Then we would lie on our backs and look up at the stars, waiting for one to streak across the sky so we could make a wish,'' Beverly continued the story.

''Tyler would always try to count them,'' Lynn added.

''And Cal would watch for UFOs.'' Beverly laughed at the memory. She and her cousins had had so much fun together. She'd always been close to Tyler in spite of the nine-year age difference between them. And of course Lynn was her dearest friend. There had sometimes been friction between Cal and Beverly. Probably because they'd been quite similar as kids—both attractive, popular and sure of themselves.

''Remember when Cal swore he saw a UFO hovering over the lake, but everyone else missed it?''

''So we never believed him,'' Beverly agreed. ''He always did like to stretch the truth.''

''But he could do tricks on water skis that would make everyone else green with envy. I don't think he's ever felt a moment of fear.''

''Why else would he have been crazy

enough to stick it out on the rodeo circuit for so long?''

Sam came back from carrying a load of supplies down a steep pathway to the boat, which was tied to the floating dock. ''Okay, you two. You're just avoiding helping by standing around reminiscing.''

Lynn lifted a grocery bag filled with potato chips and other snacks and handed it to Sam. ''We're busy supervising.''

Sam leaned over and gave Lynn a kiss. ''Slave master. And I suppose you're going to make me drive the boat, too.''

''Of course. Why else do you think I brought you along?'' Lynn answered with an intimate smile.

''I'll drive.'' A new voice joined the conversation.

Perfect Beverly thought. *This really makes my day.*

''What are you doing here?'' she asked bluntly.

''Well, good morning to you, too.'' Jeff grinned.

Wearing only a pair of cutoff jeans and old tennis shoes, he had a kind of loose-limbed grace Beverly had to admire. He had a six-pack of cola in one hand and a canvas duffel bag slung over one broad, bare shoulder.

Her breath caught in her throat as she looked into his twinkling eyes. The reaction was so quick and unexpected that she took a step backward. Ducking inside the back of the car, she grabbed her bag and the small thermal chest that held some fresh fruit and the chicken salad for their sandwiches. Of course she'd always noticed that Jeff was an extremely handsome man. But somehow, until that moment, she had felt no attraction to him.

Stop it, Beverly, she chided herself. *You're just so anxious to fall in love that even Jeff, the lady-killer, looks good.* She turned her head, glancing over her shoulder as Jeff lifted a large ice chest out of the trunk. His arms tensed, the tendons tightening into iron cords. Obviously, his work in the oil fields had toned his body. There was a hardness and a symmetry to his muscles that dedicated bodybuilders would kill for.

The shorts rode low on his slim hips, revealing a tantalizing line of curly dark hair that began just above his navel and disappeared into his waistband. His legs were long and almost as tanned as his chest. Even though she'd often seen him in white tennis shorts as he instructed the guests at the Hole in the Wall, Beverly had never noticed just how well developed his body was.

At that moment, he looked up and caught her studying him. Impudently, he gave her a slow, roguish wink.

God, he was insufferable! Did he think every woman in the world was attracted to him? Beverly gave an audible snort. But as he turned away, he hoisted the ice chest higher and sent the layers of bulging muscles across his back into motion. Beverly found she couldn't tear her gaze away. Looking didn't hurt, she reasoned. At least she would never succumb to his flirtations. She wasn't that desperate.

IRONICALLY, not even Jeff knew why he was there. He had no reason to join this little outing and every reason to avoid it. Although he'd struck up an easy friendship with Cal McKinney, he'd never really gotten to know

Lynn or her dentist boyfriend. And what he knew of Beverly, his survival instincts told him to avoid.

He'd been filling in for the tennis pro at the Hole in the Wall for about a month now. Scott had originally given him a job as a ranch hand, but Jeff had shown no aptitude for the work. In fact, Jeff had already told Scott he would be leaving as soon as the regular tennis coach returned. Now that he and Scott had mended a few of the bigger conflicts between them, Jeff would feel comfortable stopping for a night or two whenever he happened to pass through town on his way to his next job. But he couldn't imagine staying indefinitely with Scott and his new wife.

Just that morning, Jeff had gotten a call from Buck Dalton, one of his old friends, telling him about a new oil field that was under consideration in South Texas. He hoped Jeff could come in as a consulting partner, giving his expertise instead of a monetary investment.

Finding oil was what Jeff did best. Of course, it was a hit-and-miss situation, but until lately, his average had been higher than most. It was as if he had a sixth sense for it.

Unfortunately, the rumor had gotten around that he'd lost his touch. Since he had no idea what gave him that "touch," he was having a difficult time disproving the rumor. But this new job would give him the chance to try once more.

Why, then, was he still in Crystal Creek? It certainly wasn't because of any woman. Initially, Jeff had been attracted to Valerie, his new sister-in-law. But after the first rush of disappointment that she'd chosen his brother over him, Jeff had had to admit that he hadn't really been in love with her. He liked her and was glad they would remain friends.

He carried the ice chest to the boat and rested it on the top of the seat while he stepped over the side into the boat. He and Sam took the last of the bags from the women, then helped them get on board.

"Could you untie us?" Sam asked as he turned the key and started the powerful engine.

Jeff leaned over and slipped the ropes off

all four brass cleats, then tossed the ropes inside the boat. "All clear, captain. Anchors aweigh."

Sam eased the boat out of its cushioned stall, and soon they were motoring down the narrow inlet to the lake. Already the water was dotted with brightly colored sailboats trying to take advantage of what little wind there was, and fishermen trolling their lines, trying to find an unsuspecting largemouth bass.

"Okay, who's going first?" Lynn asked as they worked together to unpack the ski gear.

Sam volunteered and stripped to his swimsuit. Jeff took over the controls of the boat and idled the motor while waiting for Sam to get ready. The other man positioned himself behind the boat, floating in the water, his skis pointed upward at an angle and his hands firmly gripping the towrope's handle. As soon as Sam gave the sign, Jeff eased the throttle forward. The boat increased speed until Sam was on top of the water, gliding smoothly along.

Jeff's attention was divided among the RPM gauge, the skier behind the speedboat and the lake in front of them. It wasn't until he reached a steady speed that he glanced at the other occupants of the boat.

The midmorning sun was hot, and Lynn and Beverly had taken off their shorts and T-shirts and were lounging against the cushions across the back of the boat, laughing and taunting Sam.

Jeff's mouth suddenly went dry.

His gaze riveted on Beverly. God, he'd never seen anyone so beautiful. That hair, those eyes, that figure…her perfection literally took his breath away.

This wasn't the first time he'd noticed her. She was like a glowing star, brightening every room she entered and causing every red-blooded male to ache with desire.

Her hair was a rich golden color, threaded with strands of palest ash-blond. Its thick, wavy length tumbled down her back, reaching almost to her waist. As he watched the wind persistently carry it across her face, she reached inside her beach bag and pulled out an elastic, cloth-covered band. Her hands gathered the silken mass and secured it into a ponytail.

Whoa boy. Jeff forced his eyes away from the intoxicating sight. *Remember this is Beverly. Spoilt, self-centered, shallow Beverly— to whom looks are everything.* Despite his warning to himself, Jeff glanced back at her. Now that her hair was tied back, he had a much clearer view of a figure her bikini did little to hide. Jeff felt his body automatically respond to the swell of soft flesh that threatened to spill out of her skimpy top.

"He's down," Lynn yelled.

Jeff jerked his attention back to the job at hand. He steered in a wide circle and went back to where Sam was floating in the water with a ski under each arm.

"Hey, you picked up a little too much speed there, Jeff," Sam commented as they helped him climb into the boat.

"Sorry. Something distracted me," Jeff answered, carefully keeping his eyes focused away from Beverly.

"That's okay. I was getting a little tired anyway," Sam said congenially. "Who's next?"

They took turns skiing until one o'clock when Sam guided the boat back into its covered slip in front of the lake house. While the men secured the mooring, Lynn and Beverly walked up the steep path to the house.

"DID YOU SEE the way he was looking at you?" Lynn asked in a conspiratorial tone.

"Who? Jeff?" Beverly pretended surprise, although she'd been quite aware of his scrutiny.

"Oh course I mean Jeff. If it had been Sam, I'd have slugged him." Lynn unlocked the door and they walked inside the cool interior of the house.

Beverly shrugged. "Oh…Jeff looks at all women that way. You know, he reminds me of a wolf with those predatory eyes and that hungry curl to his lips. I always have the impression that he's waiting to pounce. But not on me," she hurried to add. "Jeff and I are exact opposites. We could never be attracted to each other."

Lynn smiled. While she would never deliberately hurt her cousin, she couldn't help thinking how alike Beverly and Jeff really were. Both were very attractive and somewhat self-centered. Neither seemed to have a care in the world. Lynn knew, as far as Beverly was concerned, there was another side that most people never saw. Of course, she hardly knew Jeff, so she couldn't speak for him.

"He's one gorgeous hunk. You two would make a beautiful couple, like in one of those sexy magazine ads for perfume or romantic vacations in the Caribbean."

Beverly glanced out the front window at the two men who were walking across the large deck. No, she couldn't argue with the fact that Jeff was one of the best-looking guys she'd ever seen. And he had the charm to use those looks to get anything he wanted.

"Do you want me to make the salad or the sandwiches?" Beverly asked, intentionally changing the subject.

"I'm not sure you should go into the kitchen at all," Lynn teased with a frown. "I'll never forget what you did to the home economics lab...."

"That was years ago."

"Yes, but has your cooking improved since then?"

"Well, no, but even *I* can slap chicken

salad on bread and make a sandwich.'' Beverly took her cousin's joking lightly. It was common knowledge that Beverly's talents didn't include anything remotely related to a kitchen. And the damage to the home economics lab hadn't been all *that* bad…just some smoke stains, a gutted oven and a melted pan. Of course, it had all looked a lot worse than it really was after the fire department got through flooding the room with water and foam. At least Beverly accepted that she couldn't be great at everything.

The men entered the house and Sam immediately went to Lynn and gave her a hug and a long kiss. Beverly's gaze shifted self-consciously away from them and she found herself looking directly into Jeff's eyes.

He was studying her with the same intensity he had been all day. Beverly was used to being stared at, but the way Jeff was looking at her made her uncomfortable. And it wasn't because there was anything lecherous in his manner. It was as if he was searching for something, and not quite finding it.

Beverly lifted her hands to smooth back her hair, but her fingers tangled in the wet, wavy mass. She knew she must look horrible with her soggy hair, no makeup and a shapeless T-shirt hanging down past her hips.

Jeff thought he'd never seen anything so beautiful in all his life. Beverly looked like a mermaid just pulled from the sea. For the first time he noticed something vulnerable about her.

Jeff realized that just as she now stood several steps away from Lynn and Sam, no matter where she was or whom she was with, Beverly was always standing at the edge of the group. Even when she was the center of attention, there was a distance, either physical or emotional, between her and the others.

How odd that a woman so exquisite should always be the outsider. As he continued to look at her, he saw a flicker of uncertainty in her eyes.

"Sam, be good," Lynn chided, but the affection was clear in her voice. She pushed him away with a halfhearted effort.

Beverly glanced at them, then back at Jeff. Her expression softened and she nodded toward Lynn and Sam with an indulgent smile.

Jeff felt his own lips curve in response to Beverly's compelling grin.

"Here, Jeff and I will fix the sandwiches while you two fill the glasses with ice," Beverly said, gently pushing Sam and Lynn toward the refrigerator. "I think you can handle that."

"I don't know," Jeff teased. "Love can be a powerful distraction."

"Well, since *we* don't have that as an excuse, we should be able to put together the best sandwiches ever made," Beverly responded as she flipped her long ponytail back over her shoulders.

"And I would have guessed you'd be the one doing the kissing instead of the cooking." Jeff washed his hands and joined her at the kitchen counter.

"Then you'd be wrong." She gave a mirthless chuckle.

"Hmm...do I hear disappointment? Regret?"

Beverly shrugged. "Sure, I suppose I keep wondering when it'll be my turn."

Jeff leveled a serious look at her. He watched as spots of color washed across her high cheekbones, but her eyes didn't waver from his. Jeff fought the impulse to reach out and touch her lovely face. There was a lot of pain in her expression, but it was the insecurity he saw there that surprised him. "Your turn will come, Bev."

"Well…maybe." She looked down at the container of chicken salad in her hands and focused on opening the snap-on lid. Her fingers fumbled on the tight closure and Jeff reached toward it.

"Here, let me help you with that," he said, meaning to take the bowl from her. But the second his fingers touched hers, they froze. Her skin was soft and still warm from the sun. But it was more than simply the feel of her beneath his hand. It was like a small jolt of electricity.

His gaze jerked upward, and as he met her startled eyes, he knew she had felt it, too.

They both dropped the bowl at the same instant. Being securely sealed, it bounced harmlessly on the floor, rolling to a stop between them. Jeff and Beverly bent to retrieve it, moving in awkward unison so that their hands touched again as they reached for the bowl simultaneously.

The reaction was exactly the same, except as they squatted on the floor, their faces were in much closer proximity. He could hear a faint gasp as she inhaled through slightly parted lips. He focused on those lips and felt his own breath catch in his throat. God, what gorgeous lips. Full, soft and a delicious shade of rose, those lips were made to be savored.

The rattle of ice cubes brought him back to his senses. He even managed a shaky grin as he picked up the bowl and stood. "I guess it should be stirred enough."

Beverly rose, too, and began laying out the slices of bread. "Lettie Mae makes the best chicken salad this side of the Mississippi."

She took a knife out of a drawer and began to spread chicken salad on the first slice of bread. Jeff decided he dared not chance another encounter until he'd had time to recover from the last two, so he concentrated on opening the bags of chips.

Lynn and Sam, with much more whispering and intimate giggling than was absolutely necessary, finally got the glasses filled with ice, quickly put together a green salad and carried glasses and salad to the table. Jeff took the chips and Beverly followed with a platter of sandwiches. Everyone was famished after the morning's exercise, and they quickly filled their plates.

"So, I thought we'd take a run to the other side of the lake this afternoon," Sam began as he lifted his sandwich to his mouth. "The crowds seem to be thinner over there. We should be able to get in another five or six hours of skiing before—"

The piercing tone of his beeper interrupted. Sam picked up the small black box and glanced at the code flashing on it. "Damn," he muttered, putting down his sandwich and standing. "It's my office. Where's the phone?"

Lynn pointed across the room to a table beside the stone fireplace, and Sam hurried to it.

"A dental emergency?" Beverly asked and Lynn shrugged.

Sam put down the receiver and turned to Lynn. "I'm sorry, honey, but I've got to go in. One of my patients got his front teeth knocked out in a Little League game.''

Lynn immediately stood up. "I'll go with you, if that's all right.''

"I'll take you home,'' Jeff offered.

"No, thanks,'' Lynn responded with a smile. "Sam and I haven't been able to spend much time together lately.'' She turned back to Sam. "It won't take me but a minute to change clothes.''

"I guess I'd better change, too,'' Beverly said. "I wouldn't want to get Sam's car seat wet.''

"Oh, Jeff, would you mind taking Beverly home?'' Sam asked, gathering his clothes. "I hate to ruin the day for all of us. You two stay and enjoy the sunshine. Besides,'' he added, "I really don't have time to backtrack through Crystal Creek. I need to get to Austin as quickly as possible.''

Jeff's gaze darted back to Beverly. There was a panicky expression in her eyes that very closely reflected his own feelings. But they really had no choice.

"I'd be glad to,'' Jeff agreed, leaving it up

to Beverly to protest if she had any major objections.

With a helpless look as if her friends were tossing her into the Gulf of Mexico in the middle of a school of tiger sharks, Beverly nodded. "Sure, that'd be okay with me."

"Thanks, Bev," Lynn said, as she and Sam made for the bathroom.

Five minutes later, the door shut behind Sam and Lynn, and it was quiet. Too quiet. Beverly and Jeff still sat at the table, sandwiches still on their plates.

At last Beverly took a small bite and began chewing with deliberate determination.

Jeff followed her lead and began eating.

Beverly returned the sandwich to the plate. "Pass the chips, please."

Because she hadn't been specific, Jeff handed her the bags of all three varieties.

"Thanks," she murmured and selected one of the bags. She shook a few chips onto her plate, then selected one with the studied precision of a jeweler choosing a perfect diamond for Elizabeth Taylor's newest necklace.

Jeff watched with breathless interest as her

straight, white teeth nibbled tiny bites of the chip. Then the pink tip of her tongue circled her lips, licking off the salt. It was all so innocent, and yet one of the most erotic gestures he'd ever seen.

He stood, so abruptly that the chair tumbled backward onto the carpeted floor. Beverly jumped as if she'd been shot.

"Sorry," he mumbled and carried his plate to the kitchen. "I guess I'm not as hungry as I thought. You go ahead and finish your meal and I'll clean up in here."

Jeff dumped the uneaten food into a garbage bag and piled the dishes in the sink. He squirted a generous amount of dish soap on top, then turned on the water full blast. "Want to take a few more runs in the boat?"

"Just you and me?" There was a startled note in Beverly's voice.

"Sure, why not? I haven't been waterskiing for years."

"Yes, but..."

Jeff's hands were submerged in the sudsy water, but he turned his head until he could see Beverly's face. "An hour ago, you were having a great time. Now you act as if I'm asking you to walk naked over hot coals. If you don't watch out, you'll give me a complex.''

Her mouth twitched into a smile. ''Yeah, like anything I could say would give *you* a complex. You're the most self-confident man I've ever met.''

His expression sobered. ''It's all an act, darlin'. How about you?''

For several seconds, Beverly's sapphire blue eyes stared into his gray-blue ones. ''I suppose I've done my share of acting, too. Sometimes, it's easier to pretend to be self-confident than it is to actually get rid of all those insecurities, isn't it?''

He grinned. ''I guess everyone has insecurities. Some people deal with them and some people cover them up. I guess you and I belong to that second group. Actually, Beverly, you and I are a lot alike. We've both gotten a lot of mileage out of our looks, which has its advantages and disadvantages. The advantages are obvious, but the disadvantage is that no one really takes us seriously.''

Still a little cautious, she studied him as

she answered, "No, they don't. So what should we do about it?"

"Well, I don't exactly have the answer to that, but I think if we put our heads together, we could think of something."

"Together...you and me?" she repeated skeptically.

"Sure, why not?" As her mouth opened to protest, he quickly added, "Nothing serious, just friends. We seem to be the only two singles left in a world full of couples. Maybe if we team up, sort of partners against this passion that's raging through Crystal Creek, we won't feel so left out."

"Strictly platonic?"

"Absolutely."

"I suppose we could give it a try. It's not like I have an overabundance of friends right now."

"Good," he said, his smile returning full force. "Then let's begin by spending the rest of the day out on the lake."

There was an intrigued sparkle in her eyes as she answered, "Sure, why not. As long as you keep your mind on the boat and don't run over anything."

"Then maybe you'd better keep your T-shirt on. That bikini you're wearing is pretty distracting."

"Ahh…but a friend wouldn't notice that."

He chuckled. "Of course a friend would notice. And it's my duty to tell you that that bikini is a hazard to the health of every man on this lake. Now wouldn't you feel bad if you caused some old guy to have a heart attack or if you distracted a skier and made him slam into something?"

"Gee, I didn't realize this friendship thing would extend to offering advice on my wardrobe."

"Oh sure, and tomorrow we can talk about your hair," he joked. "Have you ever thought about becoming a redhead?"

Beverly jerked the dish towel away from him and threatened to pop him with its fringed corner. "Don't press your luck, *pal.*"

"Okay, okay." He laughed, as he fended off her attack. "I'll stick to more generic subjects. Like, why don't you pack us a lunch while I finish these dishes."

She looked at the sandwiches he'd just

dumped into the garbage and reached for the bread to start over. "I never argue with a man who's volunteering to do the dishes. Do you want one sandwich or two?"

CHAPTER THREE

"IT'S LOOKING GOOD...damn good." The man speared another big piece of chicken-fried steak with his fork and pushed it around his plate until it was coated with thick, white gravy. "We should be drilling by the end of the summer."

"Hey, that sounds great." Jeff leaned forward and rested his arms on the table as he watched Buck Dalton shove the huge bite into his mouth. "When do you want me on site?"

Buck chewed the steak thoroughly, much longer than he had the piece before. He seemed reluctant to swallow. "Uh...that's why I wanted to meet with you today. I was just passing through Crystal Creek on my way to Danbury, and thought you'd rather hear it from me."

Jeff didn't have to hear any more to know

he was not going to like Buck's news. He
pushed away from the table and reclined
against the back of the booth with a nonchalance he wasn't feeling. His association with
Buck went back several years to when they
were both roughnecks on their first job for a
company out of Houston.

They'd spent twenty-four hours a day
working on that well. Because of their youth
and inexperience, they'd been given all the
worst jobs. They'd laid board roads over
muddy cow pastures while trying to avoid
rattlesnakes and water moccasins, so the
heavy equipment could drive across the
soggy ground. They'd carried countless
lengths of pipe up to the platform. They'd
retrieved tools that had been forgotten at the
warehouse and had driven into town for
carry-out lunches.

And, more important, they'd learned every
aspect of the drilling process. Caught up in
the excitement as the drill bits dug through
layer after layer of soil and rock, they'd
pushed exhaustion aside, catching catnaps in
the back of their pickups so they wouldn't
miss the big moment. When the well finally

came in, they'd tasted their first drops of oil and were immediately hooked.

But, eventually, they'd branched off in different directions. Jeff preferred the challenge of exploration and the variety of free-lancing, while Buck had moved up through the executive ranks until he was the vice-president of operations of PetroCo.

It was in that capacity that he sat across the table from Jeff in the Longhorn Coffee Shop on this steamy June afternoon.

And it was in that capacity that he was about to deny Jeff the job that could have resurrected his stagnant career. It would have been his ticket out of Crystal Creek, and out from under his brother's critical eye. With the petroleum industry still moving in slow motion, there weren't a lot of offers from which he could choose. In fact, this was the first project in several months that was open to outside bids. The truth of the matter was, Jeff *needed* the job.

He swirled the rapidly melting ice cubes around in his glass of cola and asked, ''Tell me what?''

''I'm sorry, Jeff, but they decided to go

with GeoTex.'' There was genuine regret in Buck's voice.

"GeoTex! That group of anal-retentive, pretentious jerks!" Jeff exclaimed. "All those geologists…all those tests. They'll delay drilling by at least a couple of months.''

''All those tests will save us a lot of time and money in the long run. We have to take as much of the guesswork as possible out of the equation before we can give it a green light.''

"Green light? What are you, an oilman or a traffic cop? You *know* I can find that oil, and for a hell of a lot less than GeoTex.''

"Hey, I have faith in you, buddy. That's why I called you earlier. But the company's been putting pressure on all of us lately. We don't have the capital to take the risks we used to. And your success rate lately hasn't been great.''

"So, I made a couple of bad calls. But I still say there was oil in those holes if they'd kept drilling.''

"We went down fifteen thousand feet on that last one.'' Buck shook his head. "Do you have any idea how much that dry hole cost us?''

''It was down there,'' Jeff repeated stubbornly.

''Maybe so. But we couldn't afford to go any deeper.''

''Yeah, but remember all the times I was right.''

Buck leveled an apologetic look at his friend. ''I know, but your methods are a little—'' he paused, obviously searching for a word that wouldn't offend Jeff ''—a little unorthodox. I've seen you in action and know that when you're hot, you're hot....''

''And when I'm not, I'm not,'' Jeff muttered.

''It's just that it's difficult to explain to a roomful of executives and bankers who've never been closer to an oil well than when they have to pump their own gas at a station, how you *feel* the oil. Companies like GeoTex offer solid facts and figures. On paper, their proposals look very impressive....''

His voice trailed away as the glass door of the café opened and Beverly walked in. With a toss of her head that sent her golden hair back from her perfect face, she seemed to light up the room. There were a few seconds of silence as all conversations were suspended. Beverly seemed totally oblivious to the effect her arrival had had, as she held open the door for Lynn, who followed her inside.

"Thank God for air-conditioning," Beverly said to Lynn in a voice so low it wouldn't have carried around the small room had its occupants not been so silent. As if on cue, the conversations resumed.

"Speaking of *very* impressive..." Buck murmured with obvious appreciation as Beverly approached them, heading toward an empty booth by the window.

She called out greetings to everyone as she passed, and everyone answered with the indulgent affection of a relative or very close friend. Actually, that was one of the things about Crystal Creek that both fascinated and repelled Jeff. On the one hand, it would be nice to belong to such a large, extended family. On the other hand, it could get very annoying not to be able to sneeze without everyone calling out a "God bless you."

Beverly's gaze drifted in Jeff's direction and—was it just his imagination?—her smile widened.

"Hi," she said. "It looks like you got a little too much sun yesterday, too."

Jeff automatically touched his sunburned nose and shrugged. "A little. You'd think with all the time I spend outdoors, my nose would get used to the sun."

"I guess it was the reflection off the water." A mischievous twinkle danced in her blue eyes as she added, "Or it could be from that blaze in the barbecue pit. We were lucky to rescue our steaks before they were consumed by the flames. I'm surprised the neighbors didn't call the fire department."

His lips stretched into a grin at her irresistible charm. He suspected he'd never seen that charm turned up to its full wattage, and he hoped he never would. If the way his body reacted to her when she was just being friendly was any indication, he hated to think how he'd feel if she ever directed that powerful charisma at him.

"You did say you liked your steaks well-done," he teased.

"There's quite a difference between well-done and burned to charcoal."

"Ahem." Buck cleared his throat in an apparent effort to draw her attention and he was rewarded with a dazzling smile.

"Hi, my name's Beverly," she said. "And this is my cousin, Lynn."

He took Beverly's extended hand and gave her a warm smile. "Actually, we met last time I was in town. I'm Buck Dalton from PetroCo. Jeff and I have worked together on quite a few jobs."

"*Worked*...as in past tense," Jeff muttered, but Buck didn't seem to notice as he continued his campaign.

"Why don't you two ladies sit down here with us," he said, sliding around in the corner booth and patting the empty spot next to him while his gaze focused charmingly on Beverly.

Her incredibly long eyelashes fluttered, then lowered as she tilted her head. "Why, thank you for the offer, but Lynn and I have a few things we need to discuss that wouldn't interest you gentlemen at all," she drawled.

Jeff shook his head and slumped against

the back of the booth. Where had the Scarlett O'Hara act come from? How many sides of Beverly had he not seen? This one, he had to admit, he wasn't particularly fond of.

Just then, Beverly looked back at Jeff and gave him a private, conspiratorial wink, then rolled her eyes. With that single, intimate exchange, she assured him that it was just as he'd thought—an act. With one last dazzling smile at the two men, she swept past them to the booth where Lynn, who was obviously used to being ignored while in Beverly's presence, was already seated.

Buck was the first to recover. "Hell, what's a babe like that doing in a hick town like this?" he exclaimed, when Beverly finally sat down and was out of their line of vision. "No wonder you've stuck around here as long as you have."

"She had nothing to do with me staying here," Jeff replied.

"Yeah, sure," Buck drawled. "And the sun's going to set in the east tonight."

Jeff knew it would be impossible to make his friend believe he hadn't spent more than fifteen minutes alone with Beverly before yesterday, so he shrugged it off.

But Buck wouldn't drop the subject. "She's gorgeous. How long did it take you to get her to bed?"

Jeff's fists clenched, but he managed to stay cool. "I told you, she and I don't have anything going on. I barely know her."

Buck gave Jeff a skeptical look. "Well, that's not like you at all. You've been here a month and haven't found out what that body looks like under those clothes?"

The image of Beverly's body, barely covered by that tiny bikini, pushed its way into Jeff's mind. Actually, the picture had been slipping in and out of his thoughts for the past twenty-four hours, but he'd have bitten his tongue off before he would admit that to Buck. For some reason—and Jeff had no idea what that reason might be—he felt compelled to defend Beverly's honor. The feeling was so unusual and so powerful that Jeff was momentarily silent.

"If you don't have any claim on her," Buck continued, completely oblivious to the turmoil raging in Jeff, "then maybe you can set *me* up for tonight. Does this bump-in-the-road place have a nice restaurant?''

''What do you mean, *nice restaurant?* I don't see any food left on your plate.'' The waitress had chosen that moment to walk up to the table and slap the bill on the red-and-white-checked tablecloth.

Startled, Buck glanced up at the middle-aged woman, but she was already walking away.

''Hell, you'd think she owned the place,'' Buck retorted.

''She does,'' Jeff informed him. ''That's Dottie Jones. She owns this café and the motel.''

''Speaking of motels, how about doing an old friend a favor, and help me get better acquainted with that sex goddess.'' He nodded toward Beverly. ''I wouldn't mind spending an extra night in this place if it could be with her.''

Before he even realized what he was doing, Jeff's hand darted across the table and grabbed a fistful of Buck's shirt. ''Leave her alone.''

Buck tried to pull away, but Jeff had a firm

hold on him. "Hey, buddy, if she doesn't belong to you, why should you care?"

As the logic of that statement sank in, Jeff's fingers slowly relaxed until he released his hold and moved back to his side of the table. Why *should* he care? He glanced over at Beverly's table and could get only a glimpse of silky golden hair, falling away from her face as she tossed back her head and laughed along with Lynn.

There was no denying that Beverly was very beautiful and incredibly sexy. Jeff wasn't immune to her obvious feminine charms. However, yesterday he'd seen something else. He knew that beneath the glossy glamorous shell was a lonely, vulnerable woman. Jeff felt no compulsion to protect that polished jewel on the outside, but he'd go down fighting to keep the fragile china doll on the inside from getting broken.

"Just leave her alone," Jeff repeated in a tone that left no doubt that he wasn't joking around.

Buck straightened his shirt, trying to smooth out the wrinkles over his chest. "Doesn't sound to me like a guy who isn't interested," he grumbled as he scooted out of the bench and stood. "I think I'll hit the road now. I can make it home by dark."

Jeff stood and held out his hand in a conciliatory gesture. "Thanks for stopping by. Just keep me in mind for future jobs."

"Sure. You know I will." Buck took Jeff's hand. "You're the same old hot-blooded roughneck," he said with a companionable smile. "It was good seeing you again."

"Yeah, you too." Jeff watched as Buck left the Longhorn and got into the black Corvette parked by the curb. It wasn't until the car turned the corner and disappeared behind the courthouse that Jeff realized his good friend had left him with the check.

He glanced at his watch and saw he still had an hour to kill before he was due back at the ranch for his afternoon session on the tennis courts. He picked up his half-full glass of cola and took it to the counter where he sat on a stool while he fished enough cash out of his billfold to pay the check.

"Couldn't help overhearing your conversation with that city boy," Earl Waddell, the grizzled foreman at Hole in the Wall said as he pulled out a cigar from his pocket. He glanced up in time to see Dottie nod pointedly to a No Smoking sign. "Damn rules," he muttered, as he put the unlit stogie in the corner of his mouth. "You'd think a grown man could do what the hell he wants."

"You can," Dottie retorted. "As soon as you pay your check and walk out the front door."

"Sassy broad," Earl said to Jeff, not really caring that Dottie could overhear his comment. "If I was a few years younger, I'd be after her like a duck on a June bug."

"If you were a few years younger, I wouldn't look at you twice," Dottie stated, with just a hint of a smile. "I like my men older and experienced."

Earl slapped his hand on the Formica counter with such force that everyone in the café looked around. "Then hell, woman, there ain't no one older or more experienced than I am, except old Hank. What're you doin' after you get off from work this evening?"

"I'm going to kick off my shoes, watch 'Roseanne' and go to bed early."

"I like that last part," Earl agreed.

"To sleep, you old goat. I need my beauty rest."

"Nah, from what I see, you're purty enough."

Dottie picked up Earl's check and tore it in half. "Okay, it worked again, you scoundrel. Compliments will get you a free meal here any day."

Earl slid off the stool and took his weathered Stetson from the hat rack by the door. With a wink at Jeff, he said, "Let's head back to the ranch, son. I need your help to load some feed into my truck." He gave a pointed glance toward the corner booth as he tugged his hat low on his forehead. "And while we're at it, I'll teach you a few ways to handle women, too."

Jeff looked over Earl's head to where Beverly still sat, sipping a big glass of iced tea. Tempting as Earl's offer was—not that Jeff thought the older man could teach him anything where women were concerned—Jeff had other, more important decisions to make.

Somehow he had to get back in the oil business. There was no denying that Buck's news had been a major blow. Suddenly, looking at Earl, Jeff thought of another wise old man he'd met here in Crystal Creek. What was it Hank Travis had told him? Something about oil and a piece of land he owned.

Maybe it was time to pay old Hank a visit.

CHAPTER FOUR

BEVERLY WALKED into the Crystal Creek Community Hospital the following morning staggering under the load of magazines and paraphernalia she'd brought for her favorite patients. Her arms were filled with large-print romance novels for Mrs. Goodwin, the elderly heart patient whose condition was worsening daily, puzzles for Jackie, a nine-year-old boy with leukemia and color books for dainty little Carrie, a four-year-old girl on dialysis because of bad kidneys. She immediately noticed the air of chaos in the corridors. Beverly made her way to the elevator with her burdens and managed to push the Up button with her elbow, then stood back to wait.

The elevator arrived with uncharacteristic speed and Beverly stepped aboard, juggling her armload so she could press the button for the fourth floor. When the doors opened to let her out, she was met with the sounds of patients' buzzers beeping at the nurses' station and a cry of joy from the station's lone occupant, Glenda Wong.

"Beverly, thank God you're here! You're a sight for sore eyes—not to mention sore feet and frazzled nerves. Are you up to bigger and better things today?"

Beverly carefully eased all the books and things in her arms onto an empty cart and grinned at Glenda. "Sure, anything short of brain surgery. I just don't think I'm up to that today."

"But anything else, right?" Glenda answered with a weak smile and stuck her tongue out at the blinking, buzzing board behind her.

"I have the feeling I'm going to be sorry I said that, but what did you have in mind? Am I moving up to the nursery? I've never spent much time around babies, you know." She surveyed the relatively deserted hallways. "Where is everyone?"

Glenda put her fingers to her forehead and rubbed her temples. "I have four nurses and three aides out with the flu—or spring fever. That can be deadly this time of year, too.''

Connie, another nurse, hurried up to Glenda and Beverly. ''I can only do so much, Glenda. It's either bedpans, clean sheets, baths or medicine. Take your pick.''

''The cavalry has arrived, Connie. Or at least a willing recruit. If you can do the scheduled vitals and the medication, I'll get Beverly started on her new career.'' Connie gave Beverly a sympathetic look and hurried off to get the tray of medicine and the blood pressure machine.

Glenda turned to Beverly. ''You don't have to worry about working in the nursery because that's about the only station that's fully covered.''

In spite of her protests, Beverly was a little disappointed. It was true that her experience with babies was extremely limited, but she'd found herself drawn to the glass-enclosed room every time she came to the hospital. She looked at Glenda. ''No babies? No magazines and letter writing either, huh?''

Glenda shook her head. ''Sorry, kid, nothing so glamorous. Think more along the lines of bed baths, bed changes and bedpans.''

''I don't know, Glenda. I've only been volunteering here for a few months, and—''

''What? You don't make your own bed? Shame on you. What kind of wife and mother will you make?'' As she spoke, Glenda guided Beverly down the hall toward the room on the end.

''Of course I make my own bed,'' Beverly declared with indignant pride.

''And you smell like you bathe,'' Glenda continued, ''so that just leaves the bedpans. Common sense should cover all you need to know along those lines.'' She stopped at the linen closet, pulled out a cart that was loaded with clean sheets, towels and cleaning products and pushed it down the hall. When they reached the end room, she parked it outside the door. ''Everything you need should be on this cart. Just put the dirty linens into the laundry bag on the end.''

''Dirty linens?'' Beverly echoed, as it began to dawn on her that her own slightly rumpled sheets and the sheets on the bed of a critically ill patient would be two entirely different experiences.

"Start here and work your way up and down each hall on this floor." Glenda gathered an armload of linens and thrust them into Beverly's reluctant arms.

"But…"

"You've been taking the volunteer classes, haven't you? By now you should have had at least some instruction on all of these things."

"Yes, but I haven't *actually*—"

"Then today's a good day to get some practice. And remember, neatness counts," Glenda added, already hurrying back toward the central desk where the noise of the buzzers continued.

"Neatness counts?" Beverly muttered. She hadn't counted on doing *real* work when she took up volunteering at the hospital. She'd thought all she would need to do was smile, hand out meals and magazines, amuse child patients and let someone else take care of the dirty work. Assuming she wouldn't really be dealing with the three B's—bedpans, bed baths and bed changes—Beverly hadn't paid much attention to demonstrations in the classes. But now she had no choice. They needed her, and she would just have to do the best job she could. She could only hope the patients would be patient.

Beverly knocked and hesitated a moment to compose herself before entering the room. There were two names on the door, neither of which Beverly recognized from past visits. With a confidence she didn't feel, she pushed open the door and swept inside. She had a sneaky feeling she was going to be earning her candy stripes today.

Instead of being welcomed warmly, she was greeted by a chorus of complaints.

"It's about time, nurse." Mrs. Leonard, the old lady in the first bed looked anxious. "I just had my foot operated on, dearie. I can't walk to the bathroom."

"Uh...I'll help you." Beverly waited until the woman had eased her legs over the side of the bed. "Here...lean on me," she told her and wrapped her arms around Mrs. Leonard's plump waist. Slowly, they crossed the few feet of bare floor to the bathroom. After waiting for the woman to settle, Beverly stood awkwardly, not knowing what she should do next. Fortunately, Mrs. Leonard spoke up.

"Now go away," she retorted. "I can't do anything with you standing there gawking at me. I'll call you when I'm through. And close the door."

Beverly quickly exited the small bathroom and found the other elderly lady looking at her expectantly.

"Good morning, Miss Wilson. How are we today?" Beverly felt like an idiot for the "we," but justified it because that was the way the nurses talked to the patients on "General Hospital".

"I don't know about *you,* but *I'm* used to having *my* bath right after lunch, young lady. I finished lunch more than a half hour ago. What's the holdup?" Miss Wilson fixed Beverly with a steely gaze.

"Well...I..." She heaved a deep sigh and gave the woman an apologetic look. "I'm going to give it to you straight. I've never done this before, but I'll give it my best shot. So, what comes first, a bath or a bed change?"

The dragon leveled a deprecating stare on her. "The bath, of course. You wouldn't want to get clean sheets wet, would you?"

Beverly smiled at the woman. "You remind me of a teacher I had once," she said, adding the silent thought that that teacher had also been a dragon.

The woman replied with a pleased expression, "As a matter of fact, I *am* a teacher. I've taught third grade for forty years at Crystal Creek Elementary." She squinted near-sightedly through her round bifocals at Beverly. "You know, I think I recognize you, too."

Beverly was momentarily speechless as she studied the woman. "You are *that* Miss Wilson, aren't you?"

When the old lady nodded with obvious delight at being remembered, Beverly asked, "But how on earth could you remember me? You must have had hundreds of students over the years."

"I'll admit that some of the students' faces and names have blurred. But I remember you as clear as day, Beverly Townsend."

Beverly started to protest modestly, expecting her old teacher to mention what a lovely child she'd been.

"You were a holy terror," Miss Wilson continued, clearly enjoying the memories. "You always wanted to be first in line. And when someone else's drawing won first place in the art contest, you sat in the corner and cried. When you lost that beauty contest a few years ago, I wondered how you reacted because I remembered how you used to pout whenever you didn't get your way."

"Thanks for reminding me," Beverly muttered. But she couldn't deny the truth of what Miss Wilson was saying. She'd never liked to lose, even when she was nine years old. Determined to change the subject and hesitant to try her first bed bath on an old schoolteacher, she announced loudly, "I think we'd better forgo the bath today. But I have to change the sheets."

Miss Wilson volunteered without hesitation. "Once a teacher, always a teacher. I'll teach you how to make a bed any marine sergeant would approve of."

Beverly proved to be a quick learner and finished Mrs. Leonard's bed before the elderly lady was ready to leave the bathroom. After helping her into the fresh, clean bed, Beverly changed Miss Wilson's linens while she took her turn in the bathroom. If the sheets were a little loose, neither patient complained.

"Not bad for a beginner," Miss Wilson stated in her finest schoolmarm voice.

"She did a fine job," Mrs. Leonard added. "Beverly, dear, you should consider becoming a nurse. You're so good with people."

Beverly gave them a weak smile as she began gathering up the huge pile of dirty linens from the floor. Aloud, she told them goodbye, but under her breath, she was muttering, *Me become a nurse? Not in this lifetime. I'd rather muck stalls.* Already her back was aching and she'd broken two fingernails.

She stuffed the linens in the bag on the cart, moved on to the next room and repeated the routine until she reached the end of the hallway. Parking the cart to one side she staggered to the nurses station.

"A Coke. I'd kill for a Diet Coke."

Glenda looked up from her stack of charts. "Ready for a break, Bev?"

"You mean we have time to take one?" Beverly was decidedly relieved. "What about all the other patients?" Her sigh was tired, but she managed a smile.

Glenda smiled back. "We were able to call in a few temporaries, and some other nurses and aides volunteered to come in early. But don't look too relieved. We still need you. But first, we deserve a break. Let's go down to the dining room."

"You're on." After Glenda turned the desk over to Connie, the two women started toward the elevators.

"This will have to be quick, Bev. We have to be back before the dinner trays arrive so we can pass them out and help the people who can't feed themselves. After dinner, all the water jugs need to be filled and the trays picked up. Then, not coincidentally, there always seems to be a bedpan or a help-patients-to-the-bathroom rush."

"It's a vicious cycle. How can you stand to do this *every* day?" The list of upcoming duties made Beverly even more tired than she'd been before. They stopped at the rest room and freshened up before going into the cafeteria. "It's certainly different from the soap operas where nurses slink around the hospital in short, tight uniforms seducing doctors, and holding an occasional sick patient's hand until they make a miraculous recovery. Another romantic myth in the Dumpster."

"Disappointed?" Glenda put a piece of pie and a cup of coffee on her tray.

Beverly eyed the pie hungrily, but picked up a salad instead. Then she stopped at the soft drink dispenser and got a diet cola. "Of course I'm disappointed. I grew up watching all those romantic soap operas about hospitals. And, of course, I believed dozens of handsome, eligible doctors would be competing for the honor of making me a doctor's wife."

Glenda gave her a quizzical look. "Is that what you want? Is that why you volunteered?"

Beverly laughed and shook her head. "No. I volunteered because my cousin Lynn twisted my arm. She told me I needed to get more involved in my community. But I think the real reason is that she's as determined as my mother to find me a suitable boyfriend.''

''You mean you're not interested in having a doctor for a husband?'' Glenda raised a skeptical eyebrow. ''With your looks, your mother's and your cousin's dreams could come true, you know.''

''Oh, it's not that I have anything against doctors. It's just that I've already found the perfect man. He's tall, handsome and successful, perfect husband and father material.'' Beverly sighed and took a bite of lettuce.

''So when's the wedding?''

''It was last week. He married another woman. I was her maid of honor.'' Beverly shook her head and suspected her expression was as wistful as she felt.

''Did you love him very much, Beverly?''

Beverly knew the answer. She'd been considering the question for some time now. ''It's not that I *loved* him so much, because our relationship hadn't really gone that far. It was just that he *was* so perfect for me. He was everything I needed.''

Glenda took a big bite of pie, chewed it

thoughtfully and swallowed it. "But you didn't love him?"

"I would have learned to love him."

"Don't kid yourself. You might have talked yourself into believing you did, but thirty years down the road, you'd be stuck with a perfect, boring husband and no good excuse to get rid of him. Is that how you'd want to live your life?" Glenda took a sip of her coffee as she watched Beverly over the rim of the cup.

"Would that be any worse than spending the next thirty years trying to find myself? At least I'd have someone to be miserable with. Isn't that better than being miserable alone?" Beverly reasoned.

"No. Trust me, it isn't." Glenda shook her head emphatically. "I went through that with my own marriage, and let me assure you, it's twice as miserable if you're living with someone who doesn't love you or you don't love than if you're living alone." She took another sip of coffee. "What you need is for some guy to come along and sweep you off your feet. Believe me, you won't be expecting it, because he won't be a *perfect* man."

"There aren't very many *perfect* men out there," Beverly agreed.

"I doubt there's *any,*" Glenda retorted. "In fact, your Prince Charming probably won't have any of the qualities you're looking for, but he'll take you to the heights of paradise and the depths of hell." Glenda paused as she finished her coffee. "At least you won't be bored." She got to her feet and picked up her tray. "Time to get back to our floor. I hear the rattle of dinner trays. And I want to thank you for staying a little longer than usual today. You've been a real life-saver."

Beverly and the rest of the volunteers, plus the nursing staff, spent the next two hours working at a frantic pace. Beverly followed the dinner cart and delivered the meals while listening to complaints about everything from the food to the color of the floor tiles. Then she helped settle the patients for the evening.

After all her chores were done, Beverly decided she had time for one more visit. She picked up some of the items she had brought with her.

Beverly knocked on the door, but didn't wait for an invitation before tiptoeing inside the room. She peered into the semidarkness at the motionless figure on the bed, trying to see if the patient was awake.

"Beverly, I figured you'd already gone home." A frail voice barely carried to Beverly's ears.

"It was a zoo around here today," Beverly explained as she pulled a chair closer to the bed and sat down. "They needed all the help they could get." She reached out and took the old lady's bony hand. "I'm sorry I wasn't able to get by to see you earlier."

"You shouldn't be spending all your spare time with an old woman." Her pale lips moved into a shaky smile. "A pretty girl like you should be out having fun with her beau."

"You know I don't have a beau, Mrs. Goodwin. And I visit you because I *like* to, not because I *have* to."

Mrs. Goodwin's long, thin fingers squeezed Beverly's hand, but her grip was so feeble, Beverly barely felt it.

On her very first day as a volunteer, Beverly had met Mrs. Goodwin. The elderly lady had just been transferred to a room on the fourth floor after spending several weeks in intensive care, recovering from her third heart attack. Beverly had been instantly drawn to the sweet-tempered patient who never complained. Then, when she noticed Mrs. Goodwin never had any visitors, Beverly had started spending as much time as possible with the old woman, bringing her anything that would brighten her day until she could get well.

But Mrs. Goodwin didn't get better. Instead she became weaker and more fragile. Glenda explained to Beverly that Mrs. Goodwin's heart was almost totally dysfunctional. If she were younger, she could have been a candidate for a transplant. But because Mrs. Goodwin was in her seventies, with no one to fight for her and no real reason to fight for herself, all she could do was wait to die.

"Look at the beautiful flowers I got today." Mrs. Goodwin glanced toward the cheerful arrangement of Shasta daisies, roses and ferns.

"Hmm...so that secret admirer is still around?" Beverly teased.

Mrs. Goodwin's faded blue eyes twinkled, momentarily breaking through the film of pain that always clouded them.

It had become a running joke between them. Twice a week Beverly had fresh flowers delivered to Mrs. Goodwin's room, but had never admitted being the one to send them. And Mrs. Goodwin, whose mind, when not dulled with medication, was as bright and quick as ever, had guessed right away who was responsible for the flowers.

"So, how are you feeling today?" Beverly asked.

"Fine," Mrs. Goodwin answered, but the grimace that furrowed her forehead belied her claim.

"Is there anything I can get for you? Some water? Or juice?"

"No, I'm okay," Mrs. Goodwin said, but there was an unspoken question in her eyes.

"If you're not too sleepy, I brought you something special today." She didn't have to hear Mrs. Goodwin's excited reply to know the older woman had been waiting for this. Beverly reached into the bedside drawer and pulled out a cassette player. She picked up what looked like a book from the stack she had brought with her to the room, opened it and took out an audio tape. "I found something new in the bookstore yesterday. It's a romance on tape. I listened to part of it on the way over here, and it's really good. There are actors speaking the parts and music and sound effects, just like hearing a movie."

After putting the tape into the machine and turning it on, she leaned back in the chair and watched her elderly friend's expression as the story unfolded.

Ever since Beverly had found out Mrs. Goodwin loved romances, she had brought her a half dozen every time she came to the hospital. But Mrs. Goodwin's eyesight was weak, so whenever Beverly had time, she would read the stories aloud. The tapes seemed a perfect solution to keeping Mrs. Goodwin entertained when Beverly couldn't be around.

When the tape ended, Beverly tried to turn off the machine as quietly as possible because she thought Mrs. Goodwin had dozed off. To her surprise, the old woman reached out and touched Beverly's hand.

"Would you leave it here, please? I'd like to listen to it again tomorrow."

"Sure," Beverly answered, pleased that Mrs. Goodwin so obviously liked her surprise. "Listen to it as often as you want. It's yours. They had a few others, and I'll pick them up the next time I'm at the bookstore."

Mrs. Goodwin nodded and her hand relaxed as her paper-thin eyelids drifted closed. She whispered, "You're a real blessing, Beverly."

"Good night," Beverly said softly, turning away so the old woman wouldn't see the tears in her eyes. She busied herself tidying the blanket before turning off the overhead light and slipping from the room.

She called her goodbyes to the relief nurses on duty at the desk and rubbed the small of her back as she waited for the elevator. It had been a long, rough day. Beverly couldn't remember when she'd been so tired.

The elevator doors opened and she stepped inside without even noticing there was someone already there. With a sigh, she leaned against the back wall and shut her eyes as the small compartment jerked into motion.

"So you're the beautiful angel of mercy the patients have been telling me about," a deep, amused voice said, making her eyes snap open.

She turned her head, startled to find a drop-dead gorgeous man in a white coat with a stethoscope around his neck standing across from her, watching her with open curiosity. Her hand automatically rose to her hair, smoothing the loose tendrils back from her face. She could only imagine how awful she must look. Here she was, riding down in an elevator with an incredibly handsome doctor who, if his lack of a wedding ring meant anything, was not only interested, but eligible, and she looked like she'd spent the day running a marathon...and losing.

"It couldn't be me," she answered, even managing an exhausted grin. "I almost lost one patient in the sheets when I was changing her bed, and I dropped a tray of food on poor Mr. Robbins."

"Hey, those are minor infractions considering the pressure we were all under today." He tilted his head and flashed her a wide, perfect smile. "I don't think we've met." He extended his hand. "I'm Gregory Sinclair. Today's my first day here."

Beverly took his hand, briefly wishing she'd taken the time to rub on some lotion after she washed up. "Welcome to Crystal Creek. This is a wonderful hospital."

"So I've heard. I did my residency at Dallas General, but I wanted to work somewhere smaller, more personal so I could spend more time with my patients."

Beverly blinked, wondering if she had dozed off and was caught up in a dream. Surely, this man couldn't be for real.

But he went on, "I'm just getting off, too. Why don't we go someplace for a drink?"

Beverly glanced down at her wrinkled, soiled uniform and shifted to ease the ache of her exhausted feet. As much as she wanted to accept his offer, she knew she would make poor company. "I'd love to, but I can't tonight. I'm beat."

"Another time then?" He didn't appear to be the least bit discouraged by her refusal.

Beverly nodded. The elevator settled to a stop on the ground floor and Dr. Sinclair stood to one side and allowed her to exit first, then insisted on walking her to the parking lot.

As she drove off, she glanced in her rear-view mirror at the tall, attractive, *eligible* man getting into a sparkling silver Corvette convertible. Maybe her timing wasn't so bad after all. Maybe there was one perfect man left.

CHAPTER FIVE

"YOU HAVE TO RUN up on the ball, Mrs. Kramer. You're not supposed to let it bounce three times in your court before you hit it." Jeff tried not to show his irritation as the woman on the other side of the net stood several feet behind the foul line and waited for the ball to reach her.

"But if I move up, then you can hit the ball over my head."

"Then you'll just have to move around, following the ball wherever it goes," he explained. What on earth was he doing here anyway? He wasn't a tennis pro; he was an oilman. He should be standing on the wooden floor of a derrick instead of the asphalt surface of a tennis court. "That's how the game is played," he informed the woman calmly, but he could feel his nostrils flaring in rebellion. "If you just want to stand there and hit balls, I'll hook up the ball machine." *And go to a bar and get drunk while you're out here screwing around,* he added to himself.

Of course, it didn't help his concentration that a camera crew was shooting an ad on the adjacent tennis court. It wasn't the cameras that were distracting him. No. The source of his distraction was the star of the shoot—Beverly Townsend.

Dressed in an extremely short white tennis outfit with her glorious hair swirling loose around her shoulders, she was pretty enough to sell disco records to Garth Brooks.

Jeff wasn't sure what product was being promoted. It wouldn't have mattered anyway. All he could see was Beverly.

Beverly, too, was trying gamely to keep her mind on the matter at hand. But trying to ignore the tennis lesson taking place on the next court was taxing *her.*

Beverly submitted once again to the hairdresser who was making a gallant but futile effort to keep the Texas wind from blowing Beverly's hair. The makeup artist joined her, brushing yet more powder on Beverly's already well-covered skin.

"One more time, kids," came the gravelly voice of Mike, the photographer. "John, try not to look like you have morning sickness. You're supposed to be enjoying this. Remember, you have the woman of your dreams in your arms, you've just completed a rousing game of tennis, and there isn't a sign of sweat anywhere on her gorgeous body. The message here is she can go straight from the court to the bedroom without a stop in the locker room for a shower."

The male model pasted a shaky smile on his pale face and took his place behind Beverly, putting his arms around her, and attempting to nuzzle her neck. His lips were clammy against her skin and she had to force herself not to wince. This shoot was taking more acting talent than a full-length major motion picture.

John suddenly grabbed his stomach and moaned. "Where's the bathroom?"

Beverly pointed toward the clubhouse and sighed as John sprinted away. With a glance at her watch and a groan when she discovered how slowly the hours were passing, she sat down at one of the umbrella-shaded tables scattered around the tennis court area. Mike glanced at the sky and shook his head as he made his way over and collapsed loosely on the chair next to her.

"What's wrong with John?" Beverly asked. "I've never seen a man look so pained at having to put his arms around me. Doesn't he like women?"

Mike managed a dry chuckle. "That's definitely not his problem. John's a regular Lothario with the ladies. But right now he's got something else on his mind. He just got back from a shoot in Mexico. I think Montezuma's taking his revenge."

A tennis ball bounced over the fence and rolled to a stop at Mike's feet. He picked it up and turned around to throw it back.

"Dammit, if John doesn't get his act together, we're going to lose our light!" he exclaimed as he stood. "Dodie, go get the nurse and see if she can do something for John…some Alka-Seltzer or a couple bottles of Pepto-Bismol. We can't afford to lose a whole day."

The makeup girl hurried to obey his commands, and Mike tossed the tennis ball back over the fence.

Jeff caught it on the first bounce and waved his thanks.

Beverly was trying not to be obvious about watching the tennis lesson in progress, but her gaze was drawn to Jeff's lean, muscular body like a magnet. As she waited for John to return, the plump, matronly Mrs. Kramer's lesson ended and a sassy redhead, whose bosom was too large for the halter top she was wearing, joined Jeff on the court.

"I just can't seem to get any power in my backstroke, Jeff. Can you show me one more time?" The woman's whiny, flirty tone grated on Beverly's already frazzled nerves.

"It's back*hand,* Buffy. Back*stroke* is a swimming term. Okay, let's try it one more time. Try to concentrate, now." Jeff's deep, sexy voice, combined with the fact that he was standing close behind the lovely Buffy and guiding her arm in the proper position for a good, strong backhand, caused Beverly's teeth to clench.

Buffy's shrill giggle was the last straw. Beverly got abruptly to her feet and walked over to the refreshment wagon. As she sipped a cool glass of sparkling water, she called to Jeff.

"I don't think that's the back*hand* she's worried about, Jeff."

Jeff glared at Beverly and handed the tennis racket back to Buffy. "You need to practice, Buffy. I'll turn on the ball machine so you can hit a few."

Buffy smiled coyly up at him. "Could you show me again, Jeff? The racket doesn't feel right in my hand."

"You just have to get used to your racket." Jeff turned his back on her and positioned the ball machine. "Get ready," he warned before adjusting the speed and turning it on.

He walked over to where Beverly was leaning against a tree and stopped, braced his arms on each side of her, effectively pinning her in place without touching her. "What's the matter, Beverly? Jealous?"

Beverly almost choked on her drink. "Jealous? Me? Of you and Bambi?" she sputtered.

"It's Buffy," he corrected, his lips curving into a knowing grin.

"Bambi, Buffy, bimbo…" she countered, in a voice low enough for his ears only. "What difference does it make? They're all the same. I've never seen women make such fools of themselves around a man. What is it, a secret hormone in your after-shave or that come-on-I'm-a-real-stud look in your eyes?"

Jeff refused to rise to the bait. Instead, he asked suggestively, "And is it working on you?"

"I have more willpower than that." Her words were bold, but Jeff's nearness was doing frightening things to her nervous system. She had no logical explanation for why the thought of Jeff giving *private* lessons to overdeveloped bimbos like Buffy made her heart constrict in her chest. Jeff meant nothing to her, so how could she be having these feelings that did, indeed, very much resemble jealousy?

"Right." Jeff continued, the warm flirtation in his eyes replaced by silvery disapproval. "You're holding out for a country-club jock with a fat wallet and a big diamond engagement ring in his pocket. Anything cheap isn't in your scheme of things, is it?''

''At least I have ideals and goals. All you care about is your ability to sniff out oil and available, willing females. And not necessarily in that order.''

Jeff's lips relaxed back a sexy smile. ''I've turned over a new leaf. Since the last time we talked about this, I've decided that my long-term goal is to be an oil baron. And my short-term goal is—'' his gaze shifted from her eyes to her mouth ''—to kiss you.'' His last words came out in a warm caress as his lips moved closer until they pressed against hers.

She wanted to push him away and tell him never to kiss her again. She really did…but somehow her resolve didn't transmit itself to her body. Her eyelids fluttered closed and her hands rose until they clutched his biceps in what was more of a gesture of encouragement than of rejection.

What was it about this man? No wonder the women flocked to him. He had a sexuality that was almost palpable. As much as Beverly tried to resist, she, too, was affected by it. The touch of his lips or his hands or even the intensity of his eyes was enough to set off a wildfire of emotions raging inside her. Emotions Beverly had never experienced with any other man and couldn't quite define. Emotions that delighted her, yet scared her to death.

"Now that's the kind of action I need!" Mike's voice jarred both Beverly and Jeff apart. "I'm afraid John's out of the picture, so to speak. Unless you want to continue the shoot in the bathroom." Mike looked Jeff over appraisingly. "How would you like to make a few quick bucks?"

"You're going to pay me to kiss a beautiful woman?" Jeff asked, obviously amused by the offer. "Hey, I might have to rethink that long-range goal."

"You'd make a great gigolo," Beverly agreed. Her comment was meant to be sarcastic, but her voice sounded soft and breathless even to her own ears.

Mike gave her a curious glance, then turned back to Jeff. "How about it? You're already dressed like a tennis player, and you look appropriately sweaty. It won't take too long, and you'll have an extra five hundred bucks in your pocket.''

''I don't think it's a good idea, Mike,'' protested Beverly. ''Not even your skill with a camera can make the public believe that Jeff and I are attracted to each other.''

Now it was Mike's turn to look amused. ''You could've fooled me. You two were shooting off enough sparks for a Fourth of July picnic.'' To Jeff, he explained, ''Our male model is sick, and we'd like to salvage today's shoot if possible. This location is expensive, and we're operating under a tight budget. Have you had any modeling experience?''

''No, but I'll try anything once,'' Jeff answered with a shrug and a pointed glance in Beverly's direction. ''Sure, I'll do it. I can always use the money.''

''Great!'' Mike motioned to the hairdresser and makeup artist. ''Do your stuff, gang. Let's get this show on the road and get this shooting over with. I have a hangover that needs a little tender loving care. All this standing around in the sun is making *me* sick.'' He wiped his forehead on the back of his hand. "Damn, is it always this hot in Texas?"

"Only between the months of March and December," Jeff replied as Dodie rushed up, set a chair behind him and pushed him onto it. "Hey, none of that stuff," he protested as she tried to put a layer of pancake makeup on his face.

"Yeah, he's a natural beauty," Beverly said, only half in jest.

"Well, even natural beauties need help in front of the camera," Dodie declared in a tone that clearly said she would tolerate no resistance. "Now sit still and take this like a man."

"That's the problem," Jeff grumbled as Dodie spread a thin layer of foundation over his face and patted the shine off his nose with a fluffy powder puff. "Real men don't wear this stuff."

"No one will know but you and me," Beverly teased, "and, of course, *I* would *never* tell anyone."

Jeff turned his head to give her a horrified look. "You wouldn't..."

Dodie turned his head to face the front so she could comb his hair, and then used a toothbrush to tame his eyebrows. "It's just not fair for a man to have such thick dark eyelashes," Dodie commented with a shake of her curly head.

Jeff didn't know how to respond to that since it hadn't really been stated as a compliment. He felt this was above and beyond the call of duty and that, in spite of the fact that he was feeling more foolish by the second, he was being incredibly cooperative. But when the makeup artist reached for a container of blush, he slipped out of the chair and stepped a safe distance away from her. "That's it," he stated firmly. "Either they take me like this or they find another guy."

Mike hurried over and stood between the stubbornly advancing Dodie and the equally determined Jeff. "Okay, Dodie, that's fine. We want that rugged, sweaty look." Mike nodded toward Beverly. "Why don't you touch her up while I give Jeff a few tips?"

Once again, Beverly submitted to being fluffed and powdered, while Mike explained what he wanted Jeff to do.

"You're hot for her…but you're trying to keep to the business at hand. You're giving her a tennis lesson.…"

"And see what a fine teacher he is," Beverly couldn't resist commenting as Buffy missed another easy backhand shot.

Both Mike and Jeff gave Beverly a look of censure. "We want you up close and personal," Mike continued. "And try to look like you have plans for a different kind of lesson after the game. You know what I mean?"

Jeff flashed that deadly grin that never failed to send Beverly's traitorous heart fluttering. "I've got the idea. Come on, Bev, let's work on your serve." He stood and pulled Beverly to her feet. Before she could protest, he whipped his arm around her slender waist and pulled her against him until her back was plastered against his front.

Mike thrust a tennis racket into her hand and propelled the two of them to the spot on the court where the cameras were set up.

Jeff's free hand wrapped around hers on the racket and he whispered in her ear, "Now try to concentrate." His breath filtered through her thick hair and brushed against her skin like a gentle night breeze.

Damn the man…and damn her reaction to him! "You're too close," Beverly warned through smiling lips.

"Not as close as I'd like to be," Jeff returned as he crossed their arms over her chest and guided her into a smooth overhand serve, his body moving perfectly with hers.

The camera clicked and clicked and clicked. Mike moved around constantly, changing the angles, adjusting the focus, switching lenses. "This is great stuff. Keep it up."

Beverly could see that Jeff was enjoying his role. He knew his presence was annoying her, and he was deliberately pushing his luck.

It was time he was taught a lesson—one that was totally unrelated to tennis. She moved, rubbing her buttocks slowly against his groin and was rewarded to feel he was, indeed, affected by her.

"You're not playing fair," he murmured, his voice noticeably shaky.

"You're the teacher. I learned all the rules from you."

"I don't think I could teach you a thing, darlin'."

Dodie rushed up and squirted Jeff in the face with a bottle of water.

"Hey, cut that out!" he exclaimed, reaching to wipe it away, but Dodie caught his hand.

"You don't look sweaty enough," she explained.

"That's funny—it felt like I was covered with it."

"Maybe she thought you needed a cold shower." Beverly tossed him a taunting look over her shoulder.

"Relax, Beverly, and smile. We'll be done here in no time. This is really great stuff. *Great* stuff."

Mike's instructions forced Beverly back into alignment with Jeff's body.

"See?" Jeff chuckled as he nuzzled her hair. "Even Mike recognizes greatness when he sees it."

"Conceited ass!" Beverly commented.

"Beautiful broad!"

"What?" Beverly was totally unprepared

for Jeff's retort. "Didn't you hear me? I called you a conceited ass."

"I *am* a conceited ass, and you *are* a beautiful broad. And I think we'd be great together." Jeff tightened his grip around her body and turned her into his embrace for another deep kiss, forgetting that Mike was photographing his actions.

"Perfect!" Mike's triumphant shout along with more frantic clicking of his camera brought Beverly to her senses.

"It's a wrap! You guys are beautiful together. Wow! I've never seen such chemistry. I hope it comes across on film." Mike began gathering up his equipment while Dodie and the hairdresser packed their supplies. "We need you to fill out a few forms, Jeff. Your check will be in the mail in a couple of weeks. Thanks a lot! We appreciate you filling in for us."

Jeff and Beverly were still standing dazedly, the tennis racket hanging loosely from Beverly's hand and their arms around each other. When they realized their rather compromising position, they dropped their arms to their sides and took several steps apart. Beverly turned and started to hurry away.

"Bev, wait."

Beverly took a couple more steps before her feet stilled. "What do you want?"

"Hey, I'm feeling rich tonight. How about going out to dinner with me?"

She wanted to refuse. Just as much as she had wanted to push him away when he kissed her. She wanted to refuse...but somehow when she opened her mouth, she said, "Sure, but I need to go home and take a shower."

"So do I." He glanced at his watch. "How about seven o'clock? Can you get dressed in an hour?"

"What's that supposed to mean? Do you think I need major help to look decent?"

"You two are dynamite," Mike said with a laugh. "Do y'all always joke around like that?"

Jeff grinned and shook his head. "Yeah, neither of us likes getting serious."

Beverly swallowed past the lump that had suddenly and inexplicably risen in her throat and headed toward the parking lot.

"You did good today, babe," Mike called

after her. "I'll be in touch if something else comes up."

"Thanks," she answered and gave him a casual wave as she got in her car.

As soon as she was out of sight of the tennis courts, she pushed down on the accelerator. Only an hour. It took twice that long for her hair to dry. Well, she just wouldn't take the time to wash it. She was determined to be dressed to the nines and sitting on the porch when Jeff arrived.

Why had she accepted his invitation? There was no logic to spending time with him. Even if he had *any* of the qualities she was looking for in a husband, he'd made it clear he had no intention of settling down. At best, they would have a short, hot, sexy affair, dripping with a passion she'd never felt before...but still just an affair.

Beverly wanted more. So, thank goodness she wasn't attracted to Jeff. That man was dangerous. He was the worst kind of villain, the kind that would take all she had to give, then ride off into the sunset. Beverly knew better than to get involved with him. She was smarter than that. Her plans for her future didn't include Jeff or anyone like him.

But then, she doubted there was anyone else like Jeff. He was definitely one of a kind.

HE WAS LATE. Beverly sat on the porch swing, swatting mosquitoes and trying to ignore the hands of her watch as they ticked to ten minutes past seven, then fifteen, then twenty. Was there a more annoying man on earth?

A truck turned off the county road onto the driveway and wound its way around the curves until it stopped in front of the house.

''Sorry I'm late. Mike and I got to talking about our favorite islands, and the time slipped away,'' Jeff said after hopping out and approaching the porch.

Beverly bit her tongue to keep from blasting him with what she thought of him and Mike chatting about the Caribbean while she was being sucked dry by mosquitoes the size of hummingbirds.

He opened the passenger door for her, then jogged around to the driver's side. ''We have reservations for eight o'clock. We're going to have to hustle to make it on time.''

They arrived at the trendy Austin restaurant at five after eight. It was a deceptively ordinary-looking place on the outside, but Beverly had eaten there often and knew the food was excellent.

"I'm hungry for a big steak," Jeff said as he took the menu from the waiter.

"We have a delicious beef Wellington," the waiter offered, "or you could try our lamb tartare."

"No raw sheep for me," Jeff said with a decisive shake of his head. "Don't you have just a plain ol' steak? You know, maybe a thick rib-eye, medium rare?"

"I'm sorry, sir. But these are our only meat entrées. Would you like to see a wine list?"

"Sure, why not? Although I'm not sure what wine goes with raspberries and asparagus."

"Jeff!" Beverly scolded. To the waiter, she smiled and said, "Yes, André, bring us a wine list, please."

As soon as the waiter left, she leaned across the table and glared at Jeff. "Would you please act nice, or I'll ask for a booster chair for you.''

"When I asked Scott to recommend a restaurant, I assumed it would be a place that serves *real* food. What is this stuff, anyway? And look at the prices!''

"Jeff…'' she warned.

He lifted his hands. "Fine, I'll find something my poor starving stomach can tolerate. But next time we go out, *I'll* pick the place.''

"Next time? Who says there'll be a next time?''

Slowly, his lips curved into his sexiest grin. "I do.''

"Oh, you do, do you? And do you always get what you want?''

He leaned forward, resting his elbows on the table until their faces were only inches apart.

"I have hopes that I will.''

A sensual shiver of anticipation streaked through her, and Beverly abruptly sat back in her chair. "Why don't you let me order the wine?''

He leaned back with a nonchalant shrug. "Sure, knock yourself out.''

André returned and Beverly ordered the wine and her meal. It took Jeff a couple minutes longer, but he finally decided on the beef Wellington. André brought the wine and, after Beverly approved it, he poured them both a glass, then left.

"So, Bev, is your life filled with one exciting photo shoot after another?" Jeff asked, leveling his disconcerting gaze on her.

"I wish," she admitted. "But this isn't exactly a hot spot for modeling assignments. Actually, I'd like to get into the movies eventually."

"As an actress?"

"No, as a baby wrangler!" she retorted sarcastically. "*Yes,* as an actress."

"Was that your talent in the Miss America contest?"

Beverly shifted uncomfortably. The talent competition was something she'd rather forget.

"No, my acting coach didn't think I was ready."

"What did you do then? Sing? Dance? I don't think I've ever heard anyone mention it."

"Dammit, if I could sing or dance, I'd have won that contest!" she snapped. "That was always my weakest score."

Jeff seemed genuinely surprised. "You can't sing, dance or act?"

"I didn't say I couldn't act. I just said, I wasn't ready at the time of the contest."

"Okay, I stand corrected. But with all your pageant experience, I would have thought you'd be able to sing like an angel."

"I think the term my singing teacher used was that I couldn't carry a tune in a bushel basket."

She could see he didn't realize how serious her lack of talent was.

"So, what *did* you do?" he persisted.

"I did a sort of comedy act." She met his gaze defensively.

"You cracked jokes?"

"Well, not *me* exactly. I was the straight man. Dinky was the comedian."

"Dinky?"

She lowered her voice until it was barely audible. "Dinky is my dummy."

Jeff was trying very hard not to smile.

"Well, I can see where that would be most impressive."

"Are you making fun of me?"

He must have noted, at last, her sensitivity to the subject because his eyes gentled. "No, of course not. I might tease you, Beverly, but I'd never make fun of you. You're too special for that."

Beverly was momentarily speechless at the unexpected compliment. Jeff didn't pass them out lightly, so when one came out of his mouth, she was astonished. And she didn't know how to deal with it. Not from Jeff.

"Actually, if they'd let me ride my horse on stage, I would have knocked their socks off," she rushed to add, trying to hide her confusion. "Dandi was my good-luck charm all through my competitions up to the big one. All of a sudden when I hit the big leagues with the Miss Texas title, I had to scramble to come up with something acceptable, and I was a lot better at comedy than drama."

"I'll bet you were a cheerleader, weren't you?"

She nodded.

"And the school's 'most beautiful,' and 'most popular'?"

Again she nodded. "But none of those had anything to do with *me,*" she said softly.

He reached across the table and took her hand in a genuine burst of concern. "Poor Beverly. Caught in your own image. When you look in the mirror, what do you see?"

"I...I don't know what you mean," she hedged, not wanting to face the answer she would have to give.

"You know what I see?" His expression softened as he answered his own question. "I see the sad, beautiful face of a lonely woman who wants to be loved for herself rather than for her body."

Beverly's mouth opened, but she couldn't find honest words to deny any part of his assessment.

"Not that it's a bad body," he said, his grin returning as if he sensed the conversation was getting too heavy. "Combined with the brain that you don't want anyone to know about, the tart, sassy tongue and a heart as big as Texas, it's a pretty powerful package.

I don't understand how some guy hasn't wrapped you up yet.''

''I told you, there aren't any good ones left,'' she responded lightly.

''What am I—canned ham?''

She managed a shaky smile. ''No, you're just passing through.'

André arrived with their dinners and placed them in front of Beverly and Jeff with a dramatic display of his serving skills.

The conversation remained more neutral as they ate, and Beverly watched with amusement as Jeff cleaned his plate.

''Okay, I'll have to admit, that was pretty good,'' he said when every last bite was gone. ''There just wasn't enough of it.''

''You're still a growing boy.''

Jeff glanced pointedly at the food still left on her plate. ''And I suppose you're going to say that you have to diet constantly to watch your figure.''

''If I don't watch my figure, no one else will want to.''

''No wonder no one can see past your body. You won't let them.''

''What is that supposed to mean?'' she

asked, bristling at his tone. "And I suppose if I got fat, people would be able to see the *real* Beverly and like me for what's underneath all the blubber? That is, if they would take the time to look."

"You're selling yourself short, Beverly. If you start to take yourself seriously, other people will, too."

"I take myself seriously. I'm realistic when I believe that my body is my future. Any career I pursue will relate to the way I look."

"Then maybe you're pursuing the wrong careers," he said in an annoyingly calm voice.

Once again, he left her speechless. Beverly had never seriously considered any career that didn't relate to her beauty. Oh sure, she'd once toyed with the idea of becoming a veterinarian. But that had just been the dream of a child.

It struck Beverly that she'd never really decided what she wanted to be when she grew up.

CHAPTER SIX

"DOES THIS THING still run?" Jeff asked as he looked at the ancient, battered pickup truck that was parked under a tin-roofed shed on the Double C Ranch. God only knew how many hundreds of thousands of miles the antique truck had on its odometer. One thing was obvious—time had not been kind to the vehicle. Held together as it was by rust and layers of mud, its original color was impossible to determine.

"Well, it did the last time I drove it."

Jeff glanced dubiously at the tires, which were definitely showing signs of dry rot. "How long ago was that?"

Hank paused, mentally calculating before he answered, "About 1980. That's when I broke my hip and J.T. decided I was too old to drive anymore. Shoot, I was only eighty-six or -seven then."

The hood groaned in protest as they lifted it. Jeff peered at the dust-covered parts with an experienced eye. He'd done his share of fiddling with all sorts of vehicles and knew his way around the mechanical complexities of a combustion engine. "It doesn't look too bad," Jeff commented. "A little dirty, and you're going to need to replace all these hoses and belts, but we can probably have it running in a few weeks."

"A few weeks, hell!" Hank exclaimed. "I'm goin' to the library today to check some charts and maps—to compare them to my map."

"We can go in my truck."

"Nah, I need to get this baby runnin' again anyway." Hank sucked in a deep breath and straightened. Ever since he and Jeff had spent an evening talking oil and speculating on how they could put together a crew and the equipment, should there actually *be* oil on his property, Hank had gotten a new lease on life. Jeff reminded him of himself when he was much younger. And their conversation brought back the memories of his glory days. He was reveling in it.

They spent the whole morning working on the truck, cleaning the engine, changing the oil, spark plugs and filters and charging the battery. With any luck, the belts would hold until they could get into town to buy more.

When the moment came to try starting it, Hank climbed into the cab and turned the key. The engine growled several times, then sputtered to life. With a tired cough, it died, and Hank turned the key again. Jeff made some adjustments and the engine caught and smoothed out.

"Get in," Hank called.

"Why don't I drive?" Jeff offered after shutting the hood and looking in the open passenger-side window.

"Nah, I've been drivin' since before you were born. Hell, probably since before your *grand*dad was a gleam in his papa's eyes." Hank stomped on the clutch and shifted the gears with a metal-to-metal growl that raised the hair on the back of Jeff's neck.

"Needs a little transmission work, too," Hank added. "Been meanin' to get it fixed, but the mechanic in town can't find the parts. Says the truck's too old. Can you imagine that?'' He shook his head. ''Too old! Damn, I hate to hear someone say that.''

Jeff wisely decided against adding his voice to those who thought Hank was too old to still be driving *any* vehicle, much less a truck that probably hadn't been roadworthy since the sixties. That would explain why there was no Texas inspection sticker on the windshield.

Against his better judgment, Jeff got in the passenger side and slammed the door shut. It immediately popped back open.

''Oh, you gotta hold down on the handle and ease her shut,'' Hank explained. ''She's like a woman—you gotta treat her gently.''

Jeff complied and the door latched, but a generous amount of space still showed between it and the frame. Automatically, Jeff felt for a seat belt.

''You won't find any of those dang belts in here, son,'' Hank said, guessing what Jeff was doing. ''Harnesses were meant for animals, not people.''

Jeff settled for a death grip, out of Hank's line of vision, on the edge of the threadbare seat. ''Where did you say we were going?''

"To the library," Hank answered. He reached under the seat and pulled out a rolled map. Its tattered edges and yellow color testified to its age. "I've got somethin' to show you, and I thought we could look at some current geological maps of the area. This baby might be a little out of date."

Not old, just out of date. Jeff smothered a smile at Hank's understatement.

Hank returned the map to its place on the floor and gave Jeff a wrinkled grin. "I been savin' that map all these years, waitin' for one of my grandsons to take an interest in the oil business. But Cal was too busy—first gettin' his butt busted in the rodeos and then gettin' involved in the boot business. And Ty's out playin' around with grapes. Wine!" the elderly man said with a snort. "It's a sissy drink. All that sniffin' and garglin'. Hell, they should take a shot of Jack Daniel's and get it over with."

Hank pulled out onto the county road and headed toward town, punching down on the accelerator until they were traveling at ten miles over the posted speed limit.

Jeff never would have believed the old

truck capable of moving so quickly. He only hoped it didn't self-destruct right there in the middle of the road.

"Anyway, none of my blood kin care about oil like I do," Hank continued, completely oblivious to Jeff's worried glances. "They wouldn't appreciate my little secret. And even if I gave them the land, they wouldn't know what to do with it."

"You want me to help you get a well drilled?" Jeff asked, finally guessing the direction of the conversation. Hank had a tendency to wander a bit, so it was often difficult to keep up with his train of thought.

"It's there, son. I *know* it's there." Hank's bright eyes danced with excitement. "I was puttin' together the money to wildcat it when my wife died. I guess I just lost the heart for it. Then I banged up my hip and J.T. moved me, house and all, to the Double C. But the past few years, I been wantin' to get back to it. You know how it is with the oil business…I miss it."

"Yeah, I know," Jeff agreed. "I've been missing it myself. But I'm not having any luck finding a job."

"Then you've got time to go check this out with me," Hank stated.

"Well, sure, I suppose so. Where is this land?"

"In Brazoria County, just outside a little town named Alvin. Ever heard of it?"

"Other than it's Nolan Ryan's hometown, I've heard there's a few good oil fields in the area. A friend of mine who's with PetroCo is about to start a job in Danbury, which is only a few miles from Alvin."

"This one's gonna be more than just a *good* oilfield. It's gonna be a gusher that'll put Spindletop to shame."

"Have there been any tests done on it?"

"Nope, don't need 'em. The oil's there," Hank answered positively. "I can *feel* it. And once you're there, you'll feel it, too."

In spite of the overwhelming likelihood that Hank was just blowing hot air, the old, familiar rush of adrenaline at the thought of finding oil swept over Jeff.

He turned to Hank, eager to continue the discussion. But the old man's face was twisted in a strange expression. All of a sudden, Hank's gnarled fingers tightened on the wheel and he slumped forward, jerking the wheel sharply to the right.

Jeff leaped forward and tried to grab the wheel and dislodge Hank's foot from the gas pedal at the same time. But it was too late. The truck was traveling too fast as it plowed through the carpet of pink buttercups and yellow dandelions that lined the road. The ditch barely slowed them down, but the soft mud jerked the truck to the left. The vehicle slid several more yards before slamming into a three-foot-tall concrete drainage culvert.

BEVERLY SAT at Mrs. Goodwin's bedside, reading aloud from one of the romance novels the old lady enjoyed so much. Her condition had worsened to the point that Beverly could scarcely tell if she was even conscious. Only a faint smile on the woman's face when Beverly came to an especially racy scene gave her any hope at all. Finally, when the old woman's breathing became so deep that Beverly knew she was truly asleep, Beverly stood and stretched her aching back.

Her shift as a volunteer had been over an hour ago, but she couldn't bear to leave Mrs.

Goodwin. She pressed a kiss on the woman's forehead, whispered goodbye and crept out of the room.

In the hallway, Glenda ran past, obviously in a hurry. Beverly automatically fell into step, more out of curiosity than because she thought she might be of help.

"What's going on?" she asked once they were in the elevator, going down.

"There's been a bad car accident and the emergency room is understaffed, just like the rest of this hospital."

A chill chased down Beverly's spine. Since Crystal Creek was such a small community, the chances were good that she would know the accident victims. "Do you have any idea who was involved?"

"I'm not sure, but I think they said it was that old man, Hank, and a young guy...Jeff Something."

Beverly's heart leapt into her throat. Hank and Jeff? *Oh God, please don't let them be dead,* she prayed as she watched Glenda rush through the swinging doors at the end of the emergency-room waiting area.

As soon as the emergency-room nurse returned to her desk, Beverly rushed over to it. "How are they...Hank and Jeff? Do you have anything on their condition? They're not...?" She couldn't bring herself to speak the words as tears filled her eyes. It was amazing how much feeling she had for that cocky Jeff. Suddenly, all she could think about was his gorgeous smile and deep, warm laugh and the way those blue eyes studied her and how good his lips felt on hers.

The sympathetic nurse smiled and said, "They're both alive. But the old man's in bad shape. They think maybe he suffered a stroke before he lost control of his truck."

"What about Jeff?" Beverly asked anxiously.

"You know him?" the nurse answered.

Beverly nodded eagerly. "Is he okay?"

"He'll be all right. He's pretty bruised up, and he might have a couple of broken ribs. He's in X-ray right now."

Beverly breathed a sigh of relief and smiled her thanks to the nurse before hurrying to the X-ray department to await news about Jeff. She paced nervously in the sparsely furnished waiting room. Then, unable to bear the tension, she ventured up the hall to listen at the door of the X-ray room where Jeff was. Her ear was pressed against the door and she was unaware of anyone's presence until a deep voice spoke to her.

"Well, Miss Angel of Mercy. Are you working on this floor today?"

Beverly whirled around and found that she was almost nose to nose with the handsome doctor she had met in the elevator two days ago. She glanced at the door again. "I have a friend in there. I just want to know what his condition is."

"*His* condition?" A look of disappointment crossed Dr. Sinclair's face.

"Yes, Jeff's sort of an old friend of the family. I couldn't go home without knowing how he is."

"Jeff Harris?" he questioned. "I've just been assigned to his case. Let me check his X rays and I'll get right back to you. If he doesn't require emergency surgery maybe we could go get a bite to eat afterward?"

Beverly nodded. "I suppose that would be

okay. If you don't mind being seen with a lowly volunteer.''

Dr. Sinclair winked at her and disappeared into the X-ray room. In moments he was back. ''Just some badly bruised ribs and a mild concussion. We'd like to keep him under observation overnight, but he refused. Your friend's pretty hardheaded—in more ways than one.'' He gave her another big smile. ''He'll be out in a couple of minutes if you want to wait to see him. Then we can be on our way.''

Almost immediately, the doors opened and Jeff was pushed through in a wheelchair. His face, hair and jeans were splotched with mud. His shirt had been removed and already a big bruise was appearing on his right side. His swollen, blackened eyes brightened somewhat at the sight of her.

''Hi, Bev. Have you come to hold my hand and nurse me back to health?'' Jeff managed a pained grin that nevertheless was quite dazzling.

Beverly wiped a blob of dried mud off his face. ''Are you all right, Jeff?''

''I'm gonna be fine. The doc here says I

can go home. Want to give me a lift, dar-lin'?''

Dr. Sinclair stepped forward. ''Maybe I've been too hasty. Maybe I should *insist* that you stay here a couple of days for observation. I don't like the way your pupils are dilating.'' He turned to the nurse pushing Jeff's chair. ''See to it that he's admitted for the night, nurse. And don't take no for an answer.'' He then took Beverly's arm and led her away.

Jeff shifted painfully and watched the couple walk away. Just as they were turning the corner, Beverly heard him mutter, ''Well, shoot!''

GREGORY WAVED AWAY the menu that Nora Jones brought to the table and took a sip of water. To Beverly he said, ''I've spent so much time in here since I moved to town a week ago that I know the Longhorn's menu by heart.'' Then, turning to the waitress, he smiled and asked, ''How are you doing today, Nora?''

''Just fine. And how are things at the hospital? I heard ol' Hank got himself in an accident. Damn fool, driving at his age.''

Gregory ordered grilled chicken and Beverly a salad. As soon as Nora left, Gregory focused his full attention on Beverly.

"So tell me, Angel. Are you engaged, or otherwise romantically involved?"

Gregory studied her over his glass of mineral water, giving Beverly the feeling she was a specimen under a microscope. "You're certainly direct, Dr. Sinclair," she hedged.

"Please call me Gregory," he said with a charming smile. "Doctors are notoriously short of time. We have to cut to the chase, or lose out altogether. How about that young man in X-ray?"

"Jeff? Jeff and I are just friends."

"If he's not in the running, is there someone else who's special in your life right now?"

"Not a soul in sight, Dr.—er, Gregory," Beverly said lightly. "I have no serious suitors. There aren't all that many eligible bachelors left in Crystal Creek."

"I just happen to know one."

"Oh, really?" Beverly bantered back. She was on firm footing now. If ever there was something Beverly was good at, it was harmless flirting. She could certainly hold her own with the self-confident doctor. She glanced around the room, then let her eyes slowly slide back to meet his. "Where?"

"Beverly, there's a dance at the country club on Saturday night. I'm off that day, so would you like to go there for a real meal? I know it's soon, but…well, I'd like to get to know you better."

Beverly remembered the conversation she and Glenda had had the other day. Was Dr. Gregory Sinclair the one who would sweep her off her feet? She looked into his handsome face and noted each of his perfect features, the perfectly layered blond hair, the perfectly shaped sky blue eyes, the perfectly straight nose, the perfectly white teeth. And to top it all off, he was a doctor! She couldn't ask for a more stable, successful career than that.

"I'd love to go to the country-club dance with you," she said, giving Gregory a look she knew would make his mouth water. She knew, because *she* had practiced it in the mirror. Perhaps that was why she recognized the characteristic in him. It appeared she and Dr. Gorgeous were two of a kind.

Oh God, why didn't that make her happy?

"So, Beverly, other than volunteering at the hospital, what do you do with your time? Do you work anywhere else?"

"Actually, I don't have a *real* job right now, just a little modeling," she explained, reminded once more how empty her life was. "My mother owns the Circle T ranch and I help out around there, too."

"Oh, isn't that the huge ranch just north of town?"

"No, that's the Double C. The McKinney family owns that. Our place is a little smaller, about eighty-five hundred acres. We raise cattle and quarter horses."

"I don't know much about ranching. I'm just a city boy from Dallas. I went to University of Texas in Austin and fell in love with this country."

"I went to University of Texas, too. Class of '89."

"I was five years ahead of you. What was your major?"

"Business and a minor in science," she

answered. "I was thinking about becoming a veterinarian."

"And what changed your mind?"

"Oh, I was busy with the pageants and having a good time in college." She shrugged. "I guess I was like a lot of kids then, more interested in partying than in studying."

"And I'll bet you were really popular on campus," Gregory commented, studying her with an approving look. "Now *I* spent all my time studying."

"Yeah, right... I went on a few dates with some doctors-to-be, and they found time for fun."

"I would have too, if you'd been there with me."

Nora arrived with their dinners, and their conversation switched to tales of his residency.

They were about halfway through their meal when Gregory's beeper went off. He grimaced, excused himself and dashed to the telephone to check his message. When he returned, he gave her a disappointed look.

"I'm sorry, Beverly. One of my patients is having some problems. I have to go."

"Don't worry about it, Gregory. Duty calls."

"That's the glamorous life of a doctor." He smiled and shrugged. "I'll pick you up at seven-thirty sharp on Saturday. At the Circle T?"

She nodded. "I'll be ready."

He stopped at the cash register and hurried out after giving Beverly a parting wave.

Nora stopped by the table and commented, "Such a nice-looking man."

Beverly nodded. "I suppose so."

"You *suppose* so? He looked perfect to me."

"I think that's his biggest flaw."

Nora gave Beverly a look that clearly said she thought Beverly had lost her mind. "He seemed pretty taken with you."

"A lot of men are taken with me...then they marry someone else. No sense in getting too excited until they put a ring on your finger."

"Well, maybe this one will be different."

GREGORY STRODE into Jeff's room, flipping the chart as he walked. He slid to a stop when he found Jeff sitting up in bed watching television. "So, what's the emergency, Harris? Why did you have the nurse call me?"

Jeff gave the doctor a knowing grin. "Oh, I was just wondering how long you plan on keeping me in here and away from Beverly."

"Beverly told me she's not involved with you," stated Gregory.

"Oh, she's involved, all right. She just doesn't know it yet." Jeff clicked the television to another station.

"Just what are your intentions toward her?" Gregory demanded.

"Purely dishonorable. How about yours?" Jeff changed the channel again.

"We've just met. But I plan on getting to know her a lot better."

"Just keep in mind that she's one of those high-maintenance babes. She's pretty enough, but…never mind. She'd never forgive me if I told you everything."

The doctor took a step forward. "But what…"

Jeff held up both hands defensively.

''Nope! Not another word will pass these lips. Where is Bev, anyway?''

It was Gregory's turn to smile secretively at Jeff. ''Now that's for me to know and for you to find out,'' he taunted as he turned and walked out the door, leaving Jeff with the clicker in his hand and a curse on his lips, for the second time that night.

CHAPTER SEVEN

"WHAT ARE YOU DOING here today?" Glenda asked late the next afternoon, looking up from the desk as Beverly got off the elevator. "No, don't tell me, let me guess. You love it so much here, you just can't stay away."

"Wrong." Beverly shifted the two packages she was carrying to her other arm. "I just wanted to check on some of the patients. How's Mrs. Goodwin doing?"

"Not too good. Her heart stopped twice last night. She's in intensive care today."

"Oh no." Although Beverly knew Mrs. Goodwin's condition wasn't improving, she hated to think of losing her friend.

"And Jackie?" she asked Glenda.

"He went home for the weekend. His blood tests are so encouraging, we think his leukemia might be in remission."

"And how are Hank Travis and Jeff Har-

ris?'' Beverly asked with studied nonchalance.

"Hank's still in intensive care—"

"Is he *that* serious?"

"Actually, he's doing pretty well, all
things considered. Do you know that guy is
ninety-nine years old?" Glenda chuckled.
"I've never seen a man more determined to
make it to a hundred."

"So, he's going to be okay?"

"He should be. His cuts and bruises will
heal relatively quickly, but he's going to
have to take it easy for a while. He's lucky
that stroke didn't paralyze his left side. As it
is, it's just going to be weak."

"And Jeff?"

"Ah…Jeff. I think the nurses have voted
him the man they'd most like to give a bed
bath to and keep as a patient for the rest of
their lives. Is that the Jeff you're talking
about?"

Beverly rolled her eyes. "Yes, that's the
Jeff I know. What is it about that guy?
Women can't resist him."

"Is that why *you're* here today?" Glenda
gave Beverly a curious glance. "Is he your
Mr. Right?"

"Jeff Harris?" A dry, harsh sound that was a cross between a snort and a chuckle burst out of Beverly's mouth. "The only thing he's got going for him is a nice smile—"

"And a fantastic body," Glenda added. "Not to mention enough sex appeal to stop a herd of wild horses."

"Not as far as I'm concerned. Sometimes he's the sweetest, funniest guy I've ever met, and other times he's the world's biggest jerk."

"Well, around here, he's been a real joy. I just wish more of our patients were like him."

"So, which room is Mr. Wonderful in?" Beverly forced herself to ask. "I brought him a present."

"Oh, he checked out several hours ago. Dr. Sinclair seemed anxious to get him out of here for some reason. Last night he wouldn't let Jeff go, then this morning he practically kicked him out."

Beverly sighed and glanced down at the books in her hand. "So, I guess I'm out of luck. I'll just have to deliver these later."

"Well, if it isn't Crystal Creek's very own

Angel of Mercy. This isn't one of your regular days, is it? Or did you stop by to see
me?''

Beverly turned to find Gregory standing
behind her. "Oh, hi, Gregory."

Out of the corner of her eye, she caught
Glenda's curious look.

''I'm on rounds right now or I'd buy you
a cup of coffee,'' Dr. Sinclair said. He
flashed her one of his perfect smiles, pulled
his pen out of his pocket and picked up one
of the charts from the top of the desk. ''I'll
see you tomorrow night,'' he added before
heading toward the hallway.

''So, how long has this been going on?''
Glenda asked, watching the interchange with
interest. ''Is this why you're not interested in
Jeff?''

''*Nothing's* going on. At least, not yet. All
we've shared is some conversation and half
a meal.''

''Well, that's more boring than my love
life.'' Glenda glanced down at the pile of
charts. ''If you stick around any longer, I'm
going to assign you to bedpan duty again.''

''That's it, I'm gone.'' Beverly was in the

elevator before Glenda could make good her threat.

As BEVERLY APPROACHED the Hole in the Wall ranch she decided, on impulse, to drop Jeff's present off at his house.

Jeff was living in the cottage that had been Val's before the wedding. Beverly parked her car in front of the small log house and got out slowly, almost changing her mind a half dozen times between her car and the front porch. Oh well, she and Jeff *did* have moments of friendship, and this was certainly a *friendly* thing to do. Either that or she was taking this nursing business a little too seriously.

She knocked and heard a muffled thud, followed by a very distinct curse word. Almost a minute passed before the door opened and Jeff appeared, wearing only a pair of jeans with just the bottom three buttons hastily fastened.

"What are you doing here?" he asked, not attempting to mask his rudeness. In fact, he seemed to be trying to magnify it. "Was the doctor busy this evening?"

Beverly thrust the package at him and

turned around. "I don't need this hassle," she stated as she stalked across the wide, open porch and down the first step.

"Bev, don't go," Jeff said, his voice soft and full of pain. "I'm sorry. I didn't mean to snap at you."

Beverly hesitated, her foot on the second step.

"*Please* don't go," he repeated with a groan.

She turned back to see if he was playing another game, but from the grim expression on his face and the way he was gingerly holding his side, she knew he was genuinely in pain.

"Go lie down," she ordered, returning to where he was leaning against the doorjamb. "I'll get you a heating pad." She helped him loop his arm around her shoulder, and he leaned heavily on her as she assisted him across the living room and into the bedroom. It was more difficult to ease him onto the bed, but finally, he was lying on his back.

Beverly paused for a second, looking down at him. His eyes were closed and his face was pale except for two spots of color high on his cheeks. His dark hair was tousled and falling across his forehead. She reached down and ran her fingers into its thick strands, pushing them back.

His eyelids fluttered open and he looked up at her. "Your touch is so gentle. I can see why you're such a good nurse's aide."

That little heart dance she'd been expecting when Dr. Gorgeous made his move was happening now, filling her chest with a longing and an emotion she didn't want to feel. Not for this man. Not for Jeff Harris.

She jerked her hand away. "I'll be right back."

It took several minutes of rummaging through his house to find the heating pad on the top shelf of the linen closet, the bottle of pain medication the doctor had prescribed and a clean glass.

"When did you last take these pills?" she asked as she carried the supplies back into the bedroom.

"I haven't taken any," he mumbled. "I don't like to take medicine."

"Well, too bad. You're either going to take these voluntarily, or I'll have to force them down. And I know how to, too. Do you want me to show you?"

"There are *many* things I want you to show me," he said, a hint of the rogue twinkling in his eyes for just an instant. "But forcing pills down my throat isn't one of them. Here, give me those damn things."

"Now, now, cursing won't help." She handed him two pills and helped hold the glass steady while he took a drink.

He lay back down on his pillow with a groan. "This hurts like hell. I can't remember ever being in this much pain, and it's just my ribs."

"Bruised ribs can be very painful. Just be glad you didn't break anything. With a little rest, you'll feel as good as new in no time."

Jeff managed a crooked smile. "You sound just like one of the hospital staff. Bev, I think you've missed your calling."

"Yeah, and you should be a banker."

His eyes closed again, and she searched the walls for a plug for the heating pad. She adjusted the temperature and placed it carefully on the purple bruise. She tried not to stare at his broad chest and the ridges of muscles running down his torso. Bruised, battered and weak, he was still the sexiest man she'd ever seen.

She sat by his bed until the pills took effect and he was sleeping peacefully. Then, in a move that would have shocked her mother and everyone else who knew her, Beverly did something totally out of character. With a dish towel tied around her waist, she washed Jeff's dishes and tidied up the kitchen. Next she straightened the living room, his bathroom and even—careful not to disturb him—his bedroom. She did stop short of vacuuming, reasoning that it might wake him up. Besides, she was exhausted. This housecleaning was hard work.

By then she was surprised to see how late it was. Jeff was due another dose of medication in a half hour, so she decided to wait, give him the pills, then leave. That was the least a good nurse would do...or a good friend, she reasoned as she stretched out on the sofa and flipped on the television.

BEVERLY AWOKE to the smell of coffee brewing and bacon frying.

"Good morning, Sleeping Beauty," a masculine voice drawled, pulling her attention to a pair of denim-clad legs. Her gaze followed his body up to the amused grin on his bruised face. "How about some break-fast?"

Beverly pushed her tousled hair back from her face and sat up. "Thanks, but I rarely eat breakfast."

"Oh, come on. It's the only meal I can cook with any proficiency," he coaxed. "At least, have a cup of coffee with me."

She wiped the sleep from her eyes and hoped she didn't look as disheveled as she felt. She knew she should be getting home, but the coffee smelled too good to refuse. "Okay, that sounds good. Let me freshen up first."

He returned to the kitchen while she went to the bathroom, washed her face and combed her hair. Feeling somewhat more presentable, she joined him at the kitchen ta-ble. In spite of her refusal of breakfast, he had set a plate and silverware at her place beside a cup of fresh, hot coffee. Beverly looked at the platter of fluffy scrambled eggs and crisp strips of bacon, and her stomach growled.

"Sure you won't have anything to eat?" he asked as he spooned a generous portion of eggs onto his own plate.

"I guess I will," she said, giving in to her appetite. "I didn't have a chance to eat dinner last night."

"You were too busy with your patients."

Beverly helped herself to the eggs and bacon and savored her first bite. "These are really good."

"Thanks. Eggs and chocolate chip cookies are the only things my mother taught me how to cook."

"Hmm...I love chocolate chip cookies."

"I'll remember that. They say that chocolate is an aphrodisiac, you know." His eyes twinkled as he openly flirted with her.

"I've heard that. But I don't believe it."

"Then I guess I'll have to make you some of my special-recipe cookies. They'll melt in your mouth and make me irresistible."

Beverly laughed. "And with bruised ribs, you wouldn't even be able to do anything about it," she teased.

One corner of his mouth lifted into a crooked grin. "You wanna bet?"

"As your unofficial nurse, I say you require bed *rest*. In a couple of days, you'll be as good as new."

"And then you'll be willing to try my secret recipe?"

The gleam in his eyes made Beverly's breath catch in her throat. "Uh...so what were you and Grandpa Hank doing in the truck?" she asked, choosing to change the subject rather than answer his question. "The two of you have been very mysterious."

"We're talking about going into a partnership to drill a well on some property he has down near the Gulf Coast."

"Oh, that old land," Beverly scoffed. "He's been talking about that for as long as I can remember. Mother told me J.T. even financed some sort of survey down there many years ago, and it came up with nothing."

"Well, Hank's convinced there's oil there, and he wants me to check it out."

"You're wasting your time. That's been Grandpa Hank's dream, but that's all it is. I think it reminds him of his days in the oil business. I've heard he was very successful and made a lot of money. But, like most wildcatters, he lost it all in the ongoing search for one more gusher. Oilmen are like gamblers—they may strike it rich, but they have to keep dropping those dollars in the slots, looking for more, never satisfied with what they've got.''

''I guess there's a grain of truth in that,'' Jeff admitted. ''It's a constant challenge, and it does get addictive. Hank and I understand each other and can talk about the oil business for hours. He's a nice old guy, and even if it doesn't pan out, I've promised him I'd check out his place for him.''

''Just don't be too disappointed if it's all hot air.''

''Oh, well, I'm not busy right now, so I don't mind taking a trip down to see it. Besides, I have a few contacts down there I can drop in to see, and maybe get a job lined up.''

Beverly looked at him curiously. ''Still nothing, huh?''

''No, not yet.''

''So, are you going to keep working here until something comes up?''

''I've decided to stay until my birthday in two weeks. I'll be getting a small inheritance then that will tide me over until I get a job.''

For a long moment their gazes met. She could see questions and indecision in his eyes, and knew her own must contain the same confusion. They both were very aware of the sexual attraction between them, which made them view his leaving Crystal Creek with mixed feelings. In one way it would be good to have the decision made for them, but on the other hand, they would never know what they had missed....

GREGORY GUIDED Beverly through the large double leaded-glass doors of the Crystal Creek Country Club. They passed across the marble-floored entry area and waited for the hostess to show them to their table.

Pausing in the doorway, Beverly looked across the room. Dozens of tables, dressed in their crisp white tablecloths, fresh floral centerpieces, sparkling silver and pointed mauve napkins added to the elegant atmosphere. Ever since she was a young girl, she'd loved going to the country club. Her mother and father had always made it a treat taking her out for her birthday, Easter or to celebrate something special. They'd all dressed up in their fanciest clothes and ordered whatever they'd wanted from the menu. She remembered her father's deep, rich laugh and the way he'd looked at her mother. They had been so in love. When Beverly's father died, Carolyn had grieved as if her broken heart would never mend.

Beverly wanted a love like that. She wanted a man who would adore her as her father had adored her mother. She wanted a man for whom she would feel such deep emotions that she would know she would die without him.

"Are you ready, Bev?"

Gregory's hand on her elbow and his voice in her ear startled her. She'd been so deep in her own thoughts that she'd forgotten he was there. They walked into the dining room and Gregory held out her chair as she sat. He seated himself and smiled across the glowing candles at her.

"I'm glad you agreed to go out with me tonight," he said. "Seeing you at the hospital all week and barely having a chance to talk to you has made me really look forward to this evening."

Beverly looked at him, forcing herself to concentrate on the very handsome doctor. "It's been a busy week there. What with half

the staff being down with the flu and
Grandpa Hank's accident.''

''I didn't realize that old man was your
grandfather.''

''Well, no, he isn't really. Actually, he's
my cousin Lynn's great-grandfather. He's
been living at the Double C Ranch ever since
I can remember and I spent a lot of time over
there when I was younger. So it was just natural that I started calling him Grandpa
Hank.''

''He's a crusty old codger, but sharp as a
tack. Now that young guy who was with
him—''

''Gee…I sure am hungry,'' Beverly interrupted and picked up the menu. ''What's the
chef's special tonight, Danny?'' she asked
the waiter.

''The beef Stroganoff is good and we have
boneless barbecued ribs,'' Danny answered.
''By the way, it's good to see you here again,
Miss Townsend. It's been a while.''

''Thanks, Danny. It's good to get back
here. It's my favorite place to eat in Crystal
Creek, you know.''

''It must be nice growing up in a small
town and knowing everyone,'' Gregory com-

mented after they had given Danny their order and he'd headed toward the kitchen.

"It has its advantages and disadvantages."

They kept up a lively conversation as they waited and throughout dinner. Beverly relaxed and realized she was having a good time.

"How about dinner and a movie on Wednesday?" Greg asked while they dawdled over dessert and coffee. "There's a new Kevin Costner romance out, and I'll be off work early that night."

"Great...that sounds great," Beverly answered with a little too much enthusiasm.

Beverly pointed out all the landmarks of her hometown as they drove back to the Circle T. Gregory walked her to the front door.

"Would you like to come in for a drink?" she asked, not really wanting to extend the date, but not particularly eager to end it, either.

"Thanks, but I'd better not. I'm on call in a couple hours, and I'd like to get a little sleep," he answered. "Will I see you at the hospital tomorrow?"

"Yes, I'll be in after noon. I promised the kids I'd bring a rabbit in for them to play with, and I've got a few new tapes for Mrs. Goodwin.''

''I'll try to catch you then, and we'll have a cup of coffee, okay?''

Beverly nodded, then before she could react, he took her into his arms and pressed his lips against hers.

She tried to respond. She even tried to enjoy it. If there were no bells, no sirens, no shooting stars, at least there were no alarms cautioning her that it wasn't wise to fall in love with this man. This was real life, not one of the romance books that Mrs. Goodwin loved so much. There was no such thing as a perfect hero.

As if to taunt her, the image of Jeff's sexy smile popped into her mind. There was certainly no chance of a happily-ever-after ending if she didn't get over her attraction to the wildcatter.

CHAPTER EIGHT

BEVERLY WAS PLEASED to find Mrs. Goodwin's condition had improved and she had returned from intensive care to her own room.

"You're looking wonderful today," she told the woman as soon as she neared the bed.

"And you need to get glasses, Beverly," Mrs. Goodwin responded pertly, but her weak voice showed just how much her latest attack had affected her.

"Do you want me to open your blinds? It's a beautiful day, but *really* hot. They're predicting it'll get up to the mid-nineties this afternoon."

"I used to love to sit in my backyard under a big old live oak tree in the afternoons," Mrs. Goodwin reminisced. "No matter how hot it got, it was as cool as springtime under that tree. I could sit and watch my babies playing on the grass or in the garden. They were only two years apart, you know. Mary Ellen was such a pretty little thing, all blond and pink and soft. And little Charlie was always wandering off, searching for new adventures from the first moment he could toddle around.''

Beverly was used to these ramblings about the children, so she quietly sat on the chair next to the bed and listened. During the past few weeks, Mrs. Goodwin had often talked of her children and her beloved husband. Tragically she had lost them all. Her daughter had died when she was just a little girl and her son had been killed in Vietnam. Mr. Goodwin had passed away several years ago. Beverly listened sympathetically at first and then found she enjoyed the stories. The time always passed too quickly.

''Oh, do you have to go so soon, dear?'' the old woman asked.

Beverly didn't mention that she'd been sitting almost motionless for more than an hour. Instead she said, ''I'm sorry, but I've got to check on Carrie before I leave. She's the little girl I was telling you about who's on dialysis and waiting for a kidney transplant. I want you to meet her as soon as you're feeling up to it. She looks a lot like that picture of Mary Ellen you have in your locket.''

Mrs. Goodwin raised her thin, heavily veined hand to her bare throat. ''Please, Beverly, would you help me with my locket before you leave? It's in the drawer of my nightstand. They always take it off when I go to intensive care.''

''Of course I will,'' Beverly said, retrieving the antique gold locket from the drawer and looping the long chain over Mrs. Goodwin's neck.

The old lady's hand shook as her fingers closed around the large oval. ''My children...'' she whispered and relaxed back against the pillow.

Beverly pressed a light kiss on Mrs. Goodwin's forehead before hurrying off to finish her visits.

It was a pleasant surprise to discover that Jackie was back and was sitting with Carrie in the sun room. Both children greeted Beverly with big smiles.

''A friend of mine wanted to meet you two.'' Beverly sat down and placed on her lap the small suitcase she had been carrying.

She snapped open the clasps and lifted the lid, being careful to block the children's view. "I've been telling him what good patients you are." As she continued to chatter, she slipped one hand inside an opening in the back of a dummy and gripped the mechanism that would move the doll's mouth and eyes. With a flourish, she moved the suitcase to the floor and seated Dinky on her lap.

He was dressed in his usual cowboy outfit, complete with tiny fringed chaps, a red checkered shirt, a leather vest and a straw cowboy hat. His painted smile and large, rolling eyes made the children laugh even before he spoke.

"Hi, my name is Dinky," Beverly said, her lips almost still as the dummy's mouth snapped open and shut. "I'll bet you're Jackie and Carrie. Beverly's told me you are the bravest kids in the whole world."

The children scooted closer, their delighted gazes focused on the lively face of the dummy while Beverly conducted a three-way conversation between the kids and Dinky. When her father had first suggested she take up ventriloquism, Beverly hadn't been too enthusiastic. After all, how much call could there be for people who could crack jokes without moving their lips?

But she had been surprised at how much children loved her act. Once her pageant days were over, Beverly had continued giving impromptu shows whenever she was invited to speak to a group of children. Then when she began volunteering at the hospital, Dinky had become a valuable communication tool, especially with children who didn't feel comfortable talking to strange adults. It was amazing how quickly and easily the kids would open up to the dummy's cheerful prompting.

"You're looking way too healthy to be in the hospital," Beverly said, speaking to Jackie through Dinky.

The little boy's sunken eyes sparkled with excitement. "My doctor says I'm in remission. I might even get to go home soon."

"Well, that's great news!" Beverly exclaimed, momentarily forgetting to throw her voice. Quickly correcting her mistake, she lowered her tone to Dinky's husky, boyish voice and added, "I'll bet you'll be glad to get back to your own room. I'll bet you even have a Nintendo, don't you?"

Jackie nodded eagerly. "Yes, and Mom said she would buy me the new Mario Brothers game cartridge." His expression became somber as he shrugged. "I love playing baseball, too, but I'm not very strong anymore."

Beverly's heart twisted. At his young age, the child had felt more pain and disappointment than she had in her entire life. But she managed to keep her voice cheery and upbeat as she spent another half hour entertaining Jackie and Carrie, as well as a couple other children who rolled into the sunroom in wheelchairs or hobbled in on crutches.

THE LAST PERSON on Beverly's list was Grandpa Hank. She hoped he'd be awake. Both times she had tried to visit before, the old man had been fast asleep.

What she didn't expect to find was a very chipper Hank, sitting up in bed, having a lively conversation with Jeff. The discussion ended abruptly at her arrival—almost too quickly, making her wonder just what the topic might have been.

"Hello. How are you two Indianapolis 500 drivers doing today?" she asked, forcing a smile on her face. This was the first time she'd seen Jeff since...well, since she had woken up in his house last Saturday.

"I hope you brought me some clothes, so I can get out of this place," Hank declared. "I'm gettin' downright claustrophobic cooped up in this room. All this white! I hate white. Why don't they paint the walls a nice shade of blue or green, you know, somethin' that would make a fella think of the outdoors?"

"I'll put that in the suggestion box."

"And you know what else I miss," Hank continued, unable or unwilling to stop until all his complaints were heard. "I miss the smell of an animal. Everything here smells like alcohol and death." He leaned closer to Beverly. "'Cept you, gal. You smell pretty damn good. But you're the only thing in this place that doesn't stop up my nose. Give me the good, clean smell of a horse any day."

"I'll see what I can do about that, too, Grandpa Hank. I brought you a book." She handed him the package and he tore the paper off with the eagerness of a child.

"You brought me a present? Why, hell, that's mighty sweet of you, gal. *Tales from the Derrick Floor*," he read aloud. "Why, it's about the olden days of drillin'. See here, son. You'll have to read this."

"I will, Hank," Jeff agreed, flashing Beverly an approving smile. "Just as soon as you finish it."

Hank's wrinkled face was inscrutable, but the mistiness in his eyes told Beverly just how touched he was by the unexpected gift.

"I've got to get home," Beverly said. "I'm already two hours over my scheduled time and Mother has invited Vernon to dinner tonight." She paused, then impulsively reached out and rested her hand on top of Hank's. "Is there anything else I can get you before I leave?"

"Nah, I'm just fine." Hank was back in total control of his emotions and gave her a fierce stare. "You plannin' on comin' back and visitin' me again?"

Beverly returned his steady look without wavering. "Yes, I thought I would. Do you have a problem with that?"

One bony shoulder lifted in a careless shrug. "Nah, I don't suppose I could stop you anyway, could I?"

"No, sir, you couldn't."

"Then I guess I ain't goin' nowhere."

''No, sir, you're not. I'll see you tomorrow then.''

''Fine.''

The door opened and the small room instantly became filled to overflowing with McKinneys as J.T., Cynthia and J.T.'s children arrived. They all exchanged greetings with Beverly and Jeff, then crowded awkwardly around the bed.

''Well, hell,'' Hank muttered. ''You'd think I was fresh road kill and you folks was a flock of buzzards the way you're all crowded around me like this.'' He lifted his thin hands and shooed them away. ''Step back and gimme some air. All this concern ain't healthy.''

''He likes to complain, but just look at that smile,'' Lynn whispered to Beverly. She glanced at her watch. ''Wasn't your shift over an hour ago? What on earth are you doing still here? No hot date?''

Beverly picked up her suitcase and was barely able to stifle a yawn. ''I've got nothing more exciting than tucking Dinky into bed tonight.''

''Why don't you stop by the ranch later?

You've been so busy that I haven't had a chance to talk to you.''

"Not tonight," Beverly said with a tired shake of her head. "I'm beat. But I'll try to catch up with you later in the week." She gave Hank one last smile. "I'll see you tomorrow," she promised him, then added, "goodbye, everyone" and turned toward the door.

"Wait, I'll walk out with you," Jeff called.

"Don't forget, son. Go get that map." Hank's voice followed them.

"Yes, sir, I'll do that right away," Jeff replied. "I'll try to get back here later this evening."

Hank didn't answer, but they could hear the pages of his new book turning as they walked into the hallway.

"Bev, I tried to call you yesterday."

"I went to Austin with Mother and Vernon to a quarter horse auction." As she answered, she continued walking, barely looking at him—actually, barely *able* to look at him. Around Jeff, she always lost every ounce of self-confidence she had.

Jeff must have noticed her attitude and

misjudged it to be coolness. He caught her arm, pulling her to a sudden stop.

Beverly took a step backward but encountered the solid obstacle of a white corridor wall. Jeff took advantage of her position and braced an arm on either side of her head, effectively blocking her escape. Little did he know that, when he was this close to her, escape was the *last* thing on her mind.

"Beverly, what are you still doing here…?" Glenda's voice trailed off. "Whoops, did I interrupt something?"

"Uh…no," Jeff said, moving away a little and letting his hands drop to his sides—but not before he trailed his fingers down Beverly's arms. "I was just about to ask Beverly to have dinner with me on Wednesday night."

"Uh…I can't that night," she answered. "I already have a date."

Jeff exclaimed. "Don't tell me you're going out with Dr. Kildare again."

"It's Dr. Sinclair, and I—well…" Beverly hedged. But her lack of an answer was apparently all the answer Jeff needed. A chill chased the tenderness from his eyes.

"Never mind, I forgot I already had plans

for Wednesday,'' Jeff said in a flat mono-
tone. ''See you around, Bev.''

*Why don't you ask me out for Thursday or
Friday or any other damn day of the week?*
she wanted to call after him. Of all the
luck...the first two real dates she'd been
asked for in a month, and they had to be on
the same night!

JEFF'S PATIENCE was particularly thin that afternoon as he tried to teach the proper way
to serve to a teenage girl who was more concerned with attracting the attention of a
young wrangler.

''Karen, you have to toss the ball higher
and follow through. Watch me...again.''

The girl fluffed her hair and licked her lips
as she struck a pose. ''Yeah, sure, Mr. Harris. I'm watching.''

Mr. Harris! Lord, that sounded old. He
wondered how old she thought he was, then
remembered when he'd been sixteen, he'd
thought turning thirty was a fate worse than
death. And today, he felt every one of his
almost thirty years.

Frankly, even if he lived to be as old as
Hank, he would never understand women.

When he'd awakened last Saturday morning and found Beverly asleep on his couch, the thought had flashed through his mind that he really wouldn't mind waking up with that woman for the rest of his life. It had gone as quickly as it appeared, but it had sneaked back in several times in the past few days.

He tossed the ball into the air and slammed the racket down so hard the ball sizzled across the net, barely missing Karen.

Karen screamed and dropped her racket in her haste to get away.

Jeff muttered an oath and walked around the net to pick up the racket. He was sure Scott would hear about this one. And then Scott would feel compelled to discuss it with Jeff, who was bored beyond words with his stint as tennis pro.

Obviously, it was time he moved on. He'd hung around Crystal Creek longer than he'd planned. Surely, once he hit the road, a job would open up for him. There was certainly nothing…or no one…holding him here. His birthday was in two weeks. After that he'd be gone, following the Texas wind once more.

He was in the shower when he remembered his promise to Hank.

A promise was a promise. Jeff knew Hank wouldn't rest easy until that map was recovered.

He drove his pickup through the wide elaborate archway marking the entrance to the Double C Ranch. As he parked outside the sprawling ranch house, he saw Cal standing in the middle of the corral, holding a lounge line and putting a nervous colt through his paces. Jeff walked over and stood watching, marveling at the silent communication Cal was telegraphing through the nylon rope to the young horse.

Cal noticed Jeff right away and waved. "Hi, you want to take a turn with this guy?"

"You've got to be kidding. I may dress like a cowboy and walk like a cowboy, but I could count the number of times I've been on a horse on the fingers of one hand."

Cal gave the rope a little jerk and the colt slid to a fidgety stop. He walked up and patted the horse's neck with his gloved hand, then unsnapped the rope from the animal's halter. "So, how's it going at the Hole in the Wall? Killed any dudes yet?"

Jeff chuckled. "Funny you should ask. I almost wiped out my first one today. And there have been others who have seriously tried my patience."

Cal's loud burst of laughter startled the colt, who circled the corral, kicking and bucking. "Sounds like you weren't cut out for public relations."

"Actually, I'm kind of soured on relations of all kinds at the moment."

"Sorry to hear that," Cal said. "This love business is a lot more fun than I ever imagined."

"Yeah, that's easy for you to say. You found a woman who has both feet on the ground. I seem to be attracted to women who have their heads in the clouds." Jeff shook his head and knew he'd better change the subject before his mood dipped below sea level. "Anyway, Cal, the reason I dropped by was to ask what y'all did with Hank's truck."

"That old piece of scrap metal? Daddy had it hauled to the junkyard."

"Which one?"

"Stan the Salvage Man's Wrecking Rodeo over on Tower Road."

"Thanks. Tell that pretty lady of yours 'hi' for me."

"Sure thing."

Jeff waved goodbye and got back into his pickup truck. He was glad he wasn't the one who would have to tell Hank about his most prized possession. Now, if only Jeff could get to the junkyard before Stan compacted the vehicle into a rusty cube.

The junkyard was surrounded by a six-foot wall, hiding its jumble of auto parts and partially dismantled vehicles from the road. Only a faded sign and an impressive number of hubcaps mounted all over the front of the building testified to Stan's business.

The man at the counter was busy taking apart a carburetor. "Can I help ya?"

"Is Stan here?"

"Nope. I'm Lou. Stan sold me the business about ten years ago. But Lou the Salvage Man doesn't have the same ring to it, don't you agree?"

Jeff would have assumed the man was making a joke, except that his dour face never changed expression. Jeff shrugged. "I'm looking for a truck."

"Just *any* truck?"

"No," Jeff answered. "A specific truck."

"Make?"

"Chevy."

"Color?"

"Rust."

"Year?"

"Uh…late thirties, maybe?" Jeff sighed. "Look, it was involved in a wreck last Thursday. I'm not sure when you would have picked it up, but you couldn't have picked up that many ancient pickup trucks since then."

"Just picked up the one."

Jeff swallowed hard, resisting the urge to reach across the counter and shake Lou. He pulled out his wallet and fished out a twenty-dollar bill. "Would you be so kind as to let me look at it?"

Lou picked up a rag that was almost as filthy as his hands and wiped off the top layer of grease before taking the bill and stuffing it into his shirt pocket. "Follow me."

They wound their way around stacks of threadbare tires and piles of corroded batteries until Jeff saw Hank's truck parked in front of the crusher. Considering its recent intimacy with a culvert, the truck was in surprisingly good shape. Well, at least it wasn't in much worse shape than it had been before the accident.

"That it?" Lou asked.

"That's it." Jeff started toward it, but Lou reached out and grabbed his arm.

"You can't go over there."

"Why the hell not?"

"Insurance. They got rules, you know."

"Look, all I want to do is get something out of the front seat. It won't take me but a few seconds, then you can get back to your...whatever it was you were doing."

"My business is selling parts. You want to buy something, I'll sell it to you."

Jeff's already stretched patience snapped. He yanked out his wallet, pulled out two more twenties and held them out. "I want to buy the whole damn truck."

"Are you kidding? It's an antique."

Jeff took out the rest of the bills and added them to the others, then with his best poker face firmly in place, stated, "Here's a hundred and forty bucks. It's all I have. Take it or leave it."

Lou squinted at Jeff, trying to guess if Jeff was good for a larger amount. Apparently deciding he wasn't, Lou nodded and took the money.

"She's all yours. For another fifty bucks, I'll tow it to your place."

"No thanks. I'll tow it myself." He wasn't sure how he would accomplish that. All he knew was that he wasn't giving that worm another dime. He didn't want to ask Cal or any of the other McKinneys for help because, until he decided what he was going to do with the truck, he didn't want Hank's relatives to know he had it. And Scott was in Austin.

Beverly. He hated to ask her, but she was the only person he could think of who would sympathize with Hank's loss. She might be coldhearted and calculating when it came to men, but she had a soft spot for the hospital patients.

Hopefully, she wouldn't be out with Dr. Marcus Welby Sinclair. Frankly, the mood Jeff was in right now, he wouldn't have minded knocking out a few of the perfect doctor's perfect teeth. In fact, it would have made Jeff's day.

CHAPTER NINE

"OF COURSE I CAN DRIVE a pickup truck. Why?" Beverly gave him a look that clearly said she thought he was losing his mind.

"Good. Then my next question is, would you let me park a vehicle on your ranch for a few days?"

"I suppose so, but..."

"Would you go with me to rescue Hank's truck?" Jeff asked, then went on to explain the whole situation to her.

"And you don't even know if the map is still in the truck?"

"Well, no. But it's more than just the map. You don't know how attached Hank is to that truck. I think it would kill him if it were crushed."

Beverly, who had just returned from a long ride, swung out of the saddle. With one hand on the reins and one hand resting on the palomino's golden neck, she nodded. "Okay.

Just let me unsaddle Dandi.'' As she walked toward the barn leading the horse, she called over her shoulder, ''You owe me one for this, though.''

It had been difficult enough for Jeff to come to her this afternoon after the scene in the hospital hallway yesterday. But she seemed determined to complicate it even more. He jogged along until he caught up with her at the barn door.

''What did you have in mind?'' He gave her a wary, but intrigued glance.

''I've decided to take Dandi and maybe one of the llamas from your brother's ranch to the hospital day after tomorrow to visit with the patients,'' Beverly explained. ''I think the kids and some of the older folks will get a big kick out of it.''

''Darlin', you never cease to amaze me.'' He flashed her a sincere grin and she answered it with a look that was almost embarrassed that she'd been caught doing something so un-Beverlylike.

''So, will you help me?''

''Sure. It sounds like fun.'' Jeff leaned against one of the heavy oak support posts and watched Beverly unfasten the buckles and swing the saddle off the horse's back. He took it from her and carried it to the tack room, where he hung it from a looped rope that was suspended from the ceiling. Returning to the post, he couldn't keep his eyes off her. As she stroked the horse's sleek hide first with a currycomb, then with a stiff-bristled brush, Beverly's body moved with a sensuous grace. Her beautiful hair tumbled over her shoulders and down her back, swaying rhythmically with each long, smooth motion.

The horse and the woman were a stunning pair, both golden, gorgeous and spirited. Jeff could well imagine that, had Beverly been allowed to ride Dandi onstage during the Miss America pageant, the judges wouldn't have been able even to consider anyone else. He'd watched her ride for several minutes before she'd noticed him, and the sight of her in the saddle, her sexy, slender body moving gracefully in perfect harmony with the animal beneath her had brought an immediate physical response from him.

Jeff refused to consider the fact that he just might be a little in love with her. That didn't fit into his plans at all. So why was he so angry at the thought of Dr. Perfect kissing, touching, loving Beverly? He, Jeff, had no idea what he would do if Beverly said she loved him. He only knew that, at the moment, he was consumed with a passion for her heart and her body that pushed aside all other considerations. And one of those considerations was that he wasn't being fair to her. She deserved much more than he could offer.

"All finished," she said after dumping a measure of grain into Dandi's feed pan. "What exactly am I supposed to do?"

IT HAD TAKEN all Jeff's powers of persuasion to get Beverly behind the wheel of Hank's truck.

"This looks dangerous. What if his brakes don't work and I ram into the back of your truck?" she asked.

That thought had also crossed Jeff's mind. "I'm really hoping that doesn't happen. We'll be traveling slow, and if you want me to pull off the road, just honk."

Still she looked skeptical, but gave a good-natured thumbs-up sign. Jeff double-checked the chain to his trailer hitch after it was fastened to the frame of Hank's truck. Then, pushing aside the map he'd retrieved from under Hank's seat, Jeff climbed into his cab and started the engine. Easing forward slowly, he watched in his rearview mirror as the chain tightened, then jerked Hank's truck forward.

Beverly grimaced, but kept her hands on the wheel as they continued moving. The front end of the truck had suffered the worst damage, and she was obviously struggling to keep it heading in a straight line behind Jeff's vehicle.

It seemed to take forever to drive the five miles to the Circle T. Making the turns was the trickiest part of the trip, as Beverly had to fight the truck's urge to wander in the wrong direction. When they finally pulled in behind the barn and stopped, she slumped forward, her head resting on the steering wheel.

"I hope you know what you're doing," she muttered as Jeff helped her out of the cab. "I don't think there's a mechanic in the world who can fix this thing. Maybe you can talk Hank into filling the back with dirt and using it for a planter."

"I've always been handy with engines and mechanical things, and I just thought it was right to give Hank the option. A man doesn't like to have his most prized possession taken away without warning."

Beverly leveled a curious look at him. "And just what is *your* most prized possession?"

For a few seconds, he was lost in the crystal pools of her intuitive eyes.

He forced his voice to sound light as he answered. "I suppose my truck is, simply because it's been my home for so many nights. I'm not really a possession kind of guy."

"No, they might hold you down."

"That's right.

For several long minutes they studied each other, silently asking questions to which neither had answers. Jeff wanted her to know that his feelings for her were different. But how could he expect her to understand when he didn't have a clue what they were? No, it was better not to say anything than to say something that the dusty Texas wind might blow back in his face.

"Would you like to stay for supper?" she asked, breaking the silence first.

Jeff was tempted. But things were getting too complicated. If Beverly only wanted to be his friend, why was she flirting with him? It was obvious that she was as attracted to him as he was to her. Then there was Gregory, the great doctor. Did she have her sights set on him? Where did Jeff fit into the picture? Or did he?

And why the hell did it matter so much? Once he was out of town, Beverly would find her Mr. Right, whether it was Dr. Kildare or some other pillar of society. So maybe it would be best if Jeff started fading out of the picture now. It was time to leave Crystal Creek...and Beverly, behind.

"No, thanks," he answered. "I've got other plans tonight."

"Oh? A date?" Was that a note of jealousy in her voice? Or was it merely curiosity? "Yes," he lied. His gaze lowered to her full, rosy lips and he wanted, more than anything at that moment, to pull her into his arms and kiss her until she begged him to stay and never leave her.

Drawing in a deep, ragged breath, he spun on his heel and headed for his truck. After shutting the door, he rolled down the window and called out, "And thanks for helping me today. What time do you want me here tomorrow?"

"About two p.m. I want to make sure I arrive between lunch and supper. The patients complain about the food, but they'd be furious if they were late for a meal."

Jeff nodded and soon was heading down the driveway toward the main road. He glanced in his rearview mirror and saw Beverly still standing by the barn, her hand lifted to shade the sun from her eyes as she watched his truck drive away.

Would she miss him? Even a little? Jeff reached up and pressed his fist against the strange ache in the center of his chest. As much as he hated to admit it, he knew her memory would be with him for the rest of his life.

BY THE TIME Jeff arrived the next afternoon, Beverly had groomed Dandi until she glowed like a new gold coin. She'd decided at the last minute to save the llama for another visit, after she saw what kind of reception Dandi got.

Jeff was in a quiet mood and had the

pained look of a man with a hangover. She didn't ask and he didn't volunteer any information about the previous evening.

When they arrived at the hospital, Beverly was glad Jeff was there. She left Dandi in the trailer until all the patients who were able to had gathered in the courtyard. Then while Jeff looked after crowd control, Beverly rode Dandi in front of them and put the horse through the set of tricks she had taught her. Instead of the worn brown leather saddle she used at the ranch, Beverly had brought the elaborate silver-studded black saddle and bridle her father had given her for her thirteenth birthday.

The children were wildly impressed, clapping and cheering and wanting to pat the "horsie." Dandi, with an intuitive patience, allowed them to tug her mane or stick their fingers into her large velvety nostrils. And while Beverly held the horse, Jeff gave each child who was able a chance to sit on that beautiful sparkling saddle while Glenda took their pictures with a Polaroid camera. Even Carrie was able to make a brief visit.

The older patients reacted with more reserve at first. But once they loosened up, they were louder and wilder than the young kids. Jeff even had to run to the store for more film as each elderly person insisted on posing for a photo with the horse *and* his or her favorite nurse's aide, Beverly.

Beverly worked tirelessly making sure everybody had a good time. *Interesting,* Jeff thought as he watched quietly. *Beverly doesn't realize that, for once, her physical appearance has nothing to do with the people's love for her.*

All afternoon, Beverly had noticed Jeff's gaze focused on her. When she caught him off guard, she was certain she saw a genuine spark of approval and...something more. A kind of wistful longing.

Or was she reading more into his look than was really there?

CAROLYN FACED her daughter across the breakfast table. ''So, how did the big date go last night?''

Beverly shrugged. ''Oh, it went okay. We had dinner at that French restaurant in Austin and saw a movie.''

''Just okay? Didn't you go out with Dr. Gorgeous?'' her mother asked, picking up on the nickname Beverly had christened him with.

"He's a nice guy." Beverly nibbled on a piece of whole wheat toast.

"Just *nice?* I would have thought there'd be a little more enthusiasm in your voice than that."

"Mama, I *am* enthusiastic. It's just that…"

"What?" Carolyn prompted after Beverly's pause lengthened.

"He's just nice," Beverly repeated.

"But I thought you were looking for a *nice,* successful man. And it probably doesn't hurt that he's very good-looking."

Beverly shook her head and shrugged in complete confusion. "He's perfect. He's exactly what I've been looking for. You're right—I should be dancing in the streets."

"You're not even *skipping,*" her mother pointed out.

"I don't know what's wrong with me. Who was it who said, 'be careful what you wish for because you might get it'? Well, that's how I feel right now."

"So, are you going to participate in the box-lunch auction at the Frontier Days celebration Saturday?'' Carolyn asked, trying to steer the subject in a more cheerful direction. "All the money is going to build a recreation center for the kids, you know."

"There's not that many bachelors left in Crystal Creek, Mama. Do you want to risk wiping out what's left of them with my cooking?''

"I thought maybe I could help you with the cooking, dear. No one ever has to know." Carolyn smiled at her daughter.

"You know that would be against the rules. Besides, anyone who knows me would guess the truth. My lack of domestic skills is common knowledge. You can't keep little things like flunking home economics a secret.''

"But Dr. Gorgeous wouldn't know," Carolyn persisted.

"He'd find out soon enough."

"Well, you should participate. It's for a good cause and it should be fun. Nobody takes it seriously. I doubt whether Dr. Gorgeous would judge a woman by her ability to make a good box lunch."

Beverly drained her coffee cup and stood. "I guess we could look at the bright side,

Mama. If I don't marry, you'll have a de-
voted daughter to take care of you in your
old age.'' She headed toward the back door.
''I'm going to take a ride. I'll be back in a
couple of hours.''

She went to the barn and saddled Dandi,
then rode toward her favorite part of the
ranch. In the far northwest corner where the
land was the hilliest, underbrush and trees
had been left untouched to form a forest that
provided a protected habitat for all the wild-
life native to that part of the state. Beverly
never went there that she didn't see whitetail
deer, a wild turkey or two, Spanish goats,
several armadillos and possums, as well as
javelinas or feral hogs. Before Scott had
found a way to keep his exotic game on the
Hole in the Wall property, other species of
deer and sheep had been crossing the fences
for the thick grass and abundant cover.

But today, as she let Dandi wander through
the forest, Beverly barely noticed her sur-
roundings. She was lost in thought. What was
wrong with her? Why wasn't she jumping for
joy over Gregory's obvious interest in her?
Had she met Gregory sooner—about a month
earlier, to be exact—she probably would

have been thrilled. He was one of the nicest, most eligible men she'd *ever* met.

But Jeff had messed things up. Why was she so attracted to him? Why did her heart always start to race when she heard his voice? Why did she wake up in the middle of the night thinking about the sound of his laughter or the way his eyes twinkled like a mischievous little boy's, then burned with a passion that heated her very soul? Damn him. Now she could no longer settle for "nice" and "eligible." She wanted that undefinable "something special."

Two hours later, she returned, no closer to an answer than she had been when she left. After unsaddling Dandi and letting her out in the pasture, Beverly went in search of her mother.

"I've decided to enter the auction, Mama. And I'm going to make the lunch myself." She even managed a little smile. "God help the poor man who bids on my box lunch."

"Consider peanut butter sandwiches, honey. I don't think anyone ever died from eating peanut butter."

"There's always a first time."

BEVERLY WALKED OUT of Mrs. Goodwin's room, and Gregory Sinclair instantly appeared beside her.

"Are you going to the Frontier Days celebration?" he asked.

"*Everyone* in Crystal Creek goes to that. Any excuse for a get-together, you know."

He gave her one of his charming smiles. "So tell me how to know which box lunch will be yours."

"That would be cheating." Beverly gave him a wry grin. "Besides, you're probably better off not knowing."

Gregory chuckled and Beverly waved as she turned away, heading toward Hank's room. She enjoyed her visits with the old man. Their sparring matches seemed to perk them both up.

She poked her head around the door of Hank's room. "Hi there. I hear you've been causing the nurses grief again."

A chuckle came from the bed. "Well, if it isn't little miss Goody Two-shoes come to spread sunshine and good cheer. I think I'm gonna be sick. Get me the bedpan, Jeff."

Beverly's head snapped around and she saw Jeff sitting by Hank's bed.

"Hi, darlin'. Where's Dr. St. Elsewhere? I can't believe you're here without him breathing down your neck. Beverly without her adoring lapdog doctor. And people say there's no such thing as miracles anymore."

"His name is Dr. Sinclair, Jeff," she corrected stiffly.

"You certainly can't fault his taste in women," Hank piped up.

Beverly pointedly turned her attention to the old man. "Thank you, Grandpa Hank. And how are you feeling today? Do you want me to have the ladies' auxiliary come and visit you?" She smiled at the old man.

"Don't you let those Bible-totin' old biddies anywhere near me, Beverly. They get within thirty feet of this room and they'll hear language that'll burn their ears off." Hank crossed his arms over his chest and glared at her.

"Did I ever tell you about the time the nurses turned me loose on their patients? Bed baths, bed changes, bedpans? They've been trying to get enough money together to bribe me into taking care of you all the time. Wouldn't that be fun?" Beverly leaned against the end of the bed, plumped his pillows enthusiastically, ignoring his grumbling at being disturbed. ''See you later,'' she sang out as she left the room.

Dr. Sinclair was waiting in the hall for her. Jeff, who had followed her out, nodded as if to say, ''I told you so.''

''Did you hear that Beverly was entering the box-lunch auction, doc? It's a B.Y.O.S.P affair,'' Jeff commented casually.

Gregory looked confused. ''B.Y.O.S.P.? I guess I'm not up on local lingo.'' He smiled at Beverly, then looked back at Jeff. ''What does it mean?''

Jeff flashed his crooked grin. ''Bring your own stomach pump.'' Before either Gregory or Beverly could respond, Jeff retreated into Hank's room.

THE FRONTIER DAYS celebration was in full swing. A marathon volleyball game that had been going on for hours had just ended, and a large group of hot and sweaty softball players had just decided the heat was too tough an opponent and were returning from the field, as the auctioneer announced that the box-lunch auction was about to begin.

As if most participants didn't already

know whose box belonged to whom, the auctioneer made all the women stand on one side of the park in front of the gazebo and the men on the other so there would be no unfair prompting. He picked up a box from the table behind him and sniffed it dramatically. "Umm…umm, does this smell good. What am I bid for this culinary delight?" He held up the box. "Do I hear five dollars?"

Beverly stood beside her mother. "I can't believe I let you talk me into this. I'm going to be so humiliated. I'm going to the refreshment stand to get a beer."

"But you don't like beer, Beverly," Carolyn reminded her.

"I've decided to develop a taste for it…in the absence of anything stronger. Maybe it'll cushion the blow when nobody buys my lunch." Beverly left Carolyn's side and made her way toward the refreshment stand.

Gregory had seen Beverly carry a pink-wrapped box to the platform and put it on the table. He'd watched as she tucked a fresh daisy into the bow. And now, as he watched her head for the refreshment stand, he noticed the auctioneer pick up the box with the daisy and put it up for bids.

The auctioneer tugged at the edge of the box, but the ribbon held it securely, so he gave it a cursory sniff. "Well, it smells interesting, anyway," he said. "What am I bid for this very attractive box lunch?"

Gregory raised his hand. "Five dollars."

"I've got five dollars," the auctioneer droned. "Who'll give me six?"

"I'll give you ten." Jeff's voice snapped Gregory's head around.

Gregory raised his hand again. "Twenty."

"Thirty," bid Jeff.

"Fifty!" countered Gregory.

The auctioneer looked at Jeff. Jeff shrugged and shook his head. The auctioneer turned and pointed at Gregory. "Sold for fifty dollars to Dr. Sinclair. One terrific lunch prepared by Crystal Creek's own Bobby Sue Warner. Enjoy yourselves, kids."

Gregory's mouth fell open as perpetually perky Bobby Sue picked up the box and headed in his direction. She grabbed his arm and dragged him toward a big shady tree. As they passed, Gregory glanced at Jeff, who gave him an innocent grin.

"You switched the daisy, didn't you?" Gregory accused in a low voice.

"Would I do something like that?" Jeff asked with a chuckle.

The auctioneer picked up the next offering, which was also wrapped in pink. "Another pretty box. Now what am I bid for this one?" He sniffed it. "Uh...I think it's peanut butter."

Some people in the crowd looked in Beverly's direction and smiled knowingly. Beverly downed her beer with a grimace and ordered another one.

"Come on, men, let's be good sports about this. It's for a good cause, you know. Someone give me a bid."

"Fifty dollars." Jeff's voice rang out, sounding extraordinarily loud in the silence.

The auctioneer quickly snapped up the offer. "Sold for fifty dollars to Jeff Harris. Good luck, Jeff. The little lady is over by the refreshment stand."

Jeff took the box cautiously and headed toward Beverly. With a grin he handed it to her.

Beverly wrinkled her nose and shook her head. "No thanks, I'm not hungry." She took another swig of beer. "You shouldn't have done that, Jeff."

"You're telling me. I don't have the fifty bucks. Hey, I don't suppose you could loan me fifty until I get my modeling check."

"I'll *give* you the fifty, Jeff, and thanks," she said, giving him a relieved smile. She looped her arm through his and led him down the row of booths. "I'll even buy you a hot dog."

"What about this?" Jeff shook the box cautiously as if afraid it might contain a bomb.

"I know exactly what we'll do with the box lunch from hell. We'll deliver it right after we have our hot dogs...and maybe some cotton candy."

"You're on, darlin'." Jeff tucked the box under his arm and they headed for the hot dog stand.

BEVERLY AND JEFF stuck their heads around the door of Hank's hospital room. The old man was watching "Wheel of Fortune" and had a sour look on his face. "Idiots! Can't get a damned easy puzzle like that. Where do they find these jerks? All they know how to do is buy vowels. It's Tumbling Tumbleweeds. Can't you see that, you fool? Humph!''

"Hi, Grandpa Hank," Beverly said brightly. "We thought you might be feeling left out because of not being able to go to the Frontier Days celebration, so we brought you a little something."

Jeff stepped forward and handed the box to Hank. "Here you go, buddy. I hope you enjoy this."

Hank looked up at them and squinted suspiciously. "Did you make this?" he asked Beverly.

"Well, sort of," she admitted, giving Jeff a significant grin.

Cautiously, as if he were examining a bomb, Hank slid the ribbon off and lifted the lid an inch at a time. When he got a good view of the contents, he tossed aside the lid and his expression brightened.

"You brought me a chili dog. Damn, that was thoughtful of you. I ain't had any decent food since they hauled me in here." He lifted out the chili dog and took a big bite. "And french fries." He rummaged around to the bottom of the box and took out an ice-cold bottle of beer.

"Now don't let the nurses catch you with that," Beverly cautioned, glancing toward the door. "They'd have my candy stripes if they found out I helped sneak that in to you."

"It'll be our secret," Hank assured her. "Here, open the beer for me, then you two git outta here and have a good time. And thanks." He gave them one of his rare smiles.

"Well, don't blame your heartburn on me," Beverly added after Jeff twisted the top off the bottle and they headed toward the door.

"I'll enjoy every minute of it."

Jeff and Beverly escaped to the elevator, hoping to be out of the building before the smell of french fries brought the nurses running. By the time they tracked down the source, the evidence would be long gone. And so would Beverly and Jeff.

They couldn't keep from laughing as the elevator doors slid shut.

"Did you see his expression when he saw that beer?" Jeff asked.

"It was a nice touch. I'm glad you thought of it."

"But you thought of the hot dog. That was really sweet, you know."

"Yes, well, I doubt he'd have appreciated my sandwich."

"You know, it seems like a long time since we ate," Jeff said, his voice suddenly lower and huskier.

As she looked up at him, her heart leaped into her throat. The laughter in his eyes had been replaced by a hunger of a different kind.

"What did you have in mind?" she asked breathlessly.

"I made a batch of chocolate chips cookies this morning. How would you like to come over to my place...and taste them?"

"I thought you'd never ask," she whispered. "It's been a long time since I've had a chocolate chip cookie."

"Then I think we should do something about that right now."

When the elevator doors opened on the ground floor, Beverly and Jeff were so engrossed in their kiss they didn't notice the crowd of people standing outside, watching with interest.

CHAPTER TEN

"MMM, THESE ARE delicious." Beverly took another bite of the cookie and held it in her mouth, savoring the taste.

They sat on the couch in Jeff's living room with a plate of cookies on the coffee table in front of them.

"You sound like you weren't sure they would be," Jeff joked. He was enjoying watching her as her eyelids drooped from the pure pleasure. "I told you chocolate chip cookies were a natural aphrodisiac."

Her eyelids fluttered open, but there was no censure in her expression. "I think you could be right."

"As a purely scientific experiment, let me kiss you, and you can tell me if it's any better," he suggested.

"I guess, in the interest of science, I'd agree to that."

The kiss was meant to be light and teasing,

but as soon as their lips made contact, the intent changed. Her mouth was soft and sweet beneath his, and the delicious flavor of chocolate served to fuel his hunger. The tip of his tongue slid around her lips, licking off the crumbs before slipping inside her mouth, touching her tongue and causing her to moan with pleasure.

His hands moved to cup her face and draw her closer and she responded by eliminating the open space between them on the couch. Her fingers slid up his arms and across the planes of his shoulders, then threaded themselves into the blunt ends of his hair at the nape of his neck. She cradled his head, subtly encouraging him not to move away.

Beverly knew she was approaching the point of no return. If she was going to stop this before they actually ended up in his bedroom, she knew she had to do it right away. But she had been wanting this for too long. Ever since the first moment she met Jeff, there had been a spark. At first, she'd thought it was hostility, but now she realized it was an animal magnetism as age-old and powerful as life itself. When his fingers slid down her neck and across her breast, lightly brushing one nipple, all thoughts of resistance scattered.

Her reaction was intense and immediate, and as his hand moved under her blouse and returned to cup her breast in his palm, her moan was muffled by his mouth. Even through the layer of lace on her bra, his fingers burned into her skin...and she wanted more. When she felt his other hand working the buttons of her blouse free, she didn't protest. All she could think about was feeling Jeff's wonderful mouth on her body.

There was a rush of cool air as he pushed open the front of her blouse. A flick of his fingers released the fastener of her bra and he lifted it, freeing her breasts to his eager lips. He kissed one nipple, gently pulling it into his mouth, then moved to the other one. Circling its hardened pink tip with his tongue, he nibbled and suckled it until Beverly thought she would explode.

Her body was beginning to ache from the desire he was creating. His hand slid under the waistband of her slacks and into her panties, until his fingers found the source of that throbbing need. He caressed her, moving his fingers back and forth over that oh so sensitive area until her body arched against his hand. In response, his finger slipped inside her, sending her to a whole new level of anticipation.

"Jeff...oh, Jeff..." she gasped.

"Beverly, I want you so much," he whispered, his voice husky as he returned to capture her lips again.

"Yes..."

He gently eased her backward until she was lying on the couch and he was stretched out on top of her. Her full breasts pressed against the soft fabric of his T-shirt, and Beverly could feel the hard, swollen evidence of his desire pushing hotly against her.

"We can't..." she somehow managed to breathe as a fragment of sanity penetrated her foggy brain.

"We were made for each other, Beverly. Feel how perfectly we fit together."

"Yes, but your ribs—"

"They're fine now. It's been more than a week." His words were breathless whispers against her lips as he continued to kiss her. "You're a candy striper. Make me feel better."

"You should be in bed..."

"Ah...good idea." He stood, and with no apparent strain or pain, lifted her into his arms. He bent his head for one more long, hot kiss, then carried her into his bedroom. Laying her on the bed, he looked down at her. "You *are* beautiful, and incredibly sexy. God, Beverly, I want you more than I've ever wanted anything in my life."

Beverly sat up and let her fingers trail over his chest and down his flat, muscular stomach to his jeans. The buttons opened easily and she eased the denim pants over his hips.

With a groan, he stepped out of the jeans and kicked them aside. He made quick work of removing the rest of his clothes, then slowly, teasingly undressed Beverly, one piece of clothing at a time, kissing and caressing her thoroughly as he went.

Finally, just as neither could stand any more, he moved on top of her and found that spot between her legs that was wet and ready for him. He stopped long enough for another deep, passionate kiss before he pushed into her aching femininity. When, at last, he was buried deep inside her, he paused, allowing them both time to savor the moment.

Ecstasy swept closer and closer until Beverly felt that tension burst within her. The room swirled around her, and when she closed her eyes she felt herself floating into the dark weightlessness of the star-studded universe. Her body tensed, automatically trying to hold on to the intensity of the feeling that was an odd mixture of pleasure and pain. She arched against him, and he thrust deeper still, pulled along by the ripples of her orgasm until she heard his ragged cry and felt the heat of his passion pumping into her.

They clung to each other, bound together for an eternity and yet strangely alone, wrapped in the padded isolation of their own personal reaction to their lovemaking. Slowly, they relaxed, returning to the solid cushion of the bed. Jeff rolled onto his side, but pulled Beverly with him, keeping her wrapped in the comfortable security of his arms and not breaking their most intimate connection until absolutely necessary.

Beverly snuggled closer, burying her face in the curve of his neck, breathing in and adoring his masculine scent. Jeff might not be the perfect man she had thought she was looking for, but she couldn't deny that he was perfectly a man. There could never be anyone else who could make her feel what she had just felt.

And now, could she ever settle for less?

"GOOD LORD! Has my watch stopped or is the world about to come to an end?" Lynn exclaimed as she led a rangy chestnut gelding out of his stall and tied him to the hitching post.

"Okay, so I don't get up early very often," Beverly admitted.

"What's so important to get you out of bed at the crack of dawn?" As Lynn spoke, she began brushing the horse's sleek reddish gold back.

"I couldn't sleep," Beverly answered and picked up a currycomb from the bucket. "Need any help?"

"That dapple gray needs some exercise." Lynn nodded toward a stall several doors down.

Beverly took a lead rope off a hook and brought the horse to the hitching post, where she began cleaning the dust and straw off his speckled hide.

"Since when do you have insomnia?" Lynn asked. "I remember when we were kids, you had the uncanny ability to fall right to sleep as soon as we went to bed. Boy, you were a real dud at slumber parties."

"Yeah, well, I'm a real dud at falling in love, too." Beverly slipped a bit into the dapple gray's mouth and pulled the bridle over his ears.

"Ah...man trouble. So, who's the lucky guy this week?"

"That's sort of the problem." Beverly smoothed the wrinkles out of the saddle blanket, then centered the lightweight racing saddle on the horse's straight back. "I need some advice from a woman who knows what love is."

"Right, like I'm the expert," Lynn snorted. "I've been in love exactly once in my life."

"Yes, but you knew it right away, didn't you?"

"Not *right* away. But I did know there was a special spark between Sam and me."

Yes, Beverly thought. She knew all about those special sparks. That was part of her problem.

"So, tell me, who's got you thinking of the L word?"

"Have you met that new doctor at the hospital?"

"The one who looks like a young Robert Redford? The one who was in a bidding war to get your box lunch? The one who zips around town in a silver Corvette convertible?" Lynn bent down and pulled the girth under her horse's belly. "Yes, I think I've heard a thing or two about him. Is he the one?"

"He's exactly the kind of man I *thought* I wanted."

"But?" Lynn prompted.

"But there's this other guy who challenges me. He doesn't let me sit back and get by on my looks. He doesn't pull any punches about telling me I should be doing something else with my life." Beverly thought of all the discussions she and Jeff had had, but also of the way he could make even a commonplace thing fun. She added, "He makes me laugh and he makes me cry."

Lynn checked the girth one last time, led the horse to a mounting block, then swung into the saddle. "Yes, but the real question is...does he love you?"

Her cousin glanced back over her shoulder

at Beverly and gave her a look that dared her to tell the truth.

Beverly sighed, amazed that it mattered so much. "He's never actually said it in so many words, but I'm sure he cares a lot about me. However, he's made it perfectly clear that he isn't in this for the long haul. No promises. No plans. Just a good time while it lasts." Beverly mounted the gray gelding and the two women rode side by side to the large oval racing track.

"And you're settling for that?"

Beverly gave a wistful sigh. "I don't have any other choices. Have you ever heard that Garth Brooks song called 'The Dance'? It's about a guy who can't regret the pain of losing his lover because at least it was fun while it lasted. He's grateful for the time they had and the memories they shared."

"This doesn't sound at all like you." Lynn stopped her horse and turned her full attention on Beverly. "You've always had such definite goals and you've never let anyone sway you from your course. What is it about this guy that tempts you to accept anything less than a wedding ring and a white picket fence?"

"I wish I could answer that." Beverly shook her head in total bewilderment. "If I knew, I could stop thinking about him all the time."

"So who is this mystery man?"

Beverly hesitated. It wasn't that she was ashamed to admit being attracted to Jeff. Rather, it was that she didn't want to put him up for comparison with Gregory. Even though he'd never know his attributes had been discussed and clinically measured, it somehow didn't seem fair to him.

"It's Jeff Harris, isn't it?" Lynn said, then chuckled when she saw she'd guessed correctly. "I thought so."

Beverly was amazed. "How did you know? Why, not even *I* would have guessed I'd be attracted to Jeff."

"Are you kidding? You should see your face when you look at him. I've never seen such a goofy look—on you, at least."

"No!" Now Beverly was amazed *and* horrified. If her feelings were that obvious, she must be the talk of the town.

"Calm down. I can see it because I know you so well," Lynn hurried to reassure her. "I haven't heard anyone else mention it, so your secret's safe as long as you want to keep it that way.''

''I don't know what I want. The only thing I'm absolutely certain of is that I don't want to miss 'the dance' with Jeff. I'll just have to deal with the pain later.''

''Then that's your answer. Have fun while you can. You'll have plenty of time to settle down later. And you'll always have the memories.''

''That's all I'll ever have. Just memories. Memories of my father. Memories of the pageants I won and the big one I didn't. Memories of falling in love with the wrong guy.''

''Yes, but like Garth said, it's better to take the chance than to miss out.''

''I just hope ol' Garth knows what he's talking about.''

''He must know something. Look how happy his marriage is.'' Lynn clucked to her horse and started him moving again. ''What's going on between Grandpa and Jeff? Each time I visit Grandpa in the hospital, Jeff's there.''

''You won't believe it, but somehow

Grandpa Hank has gotten Jeff wrapped up in that land he has down by Galveston.''

''You're kidding! I thought he'd given up on that.''

''Well, I guess the two of them just hit it off. I think oilmen live in their own little world, anyway.''

''I have to admit that it's doing Grandpa Hank a lot of good. I haven't seen him so excited about anything in years. It's given him a whole new lease on life. I just hope he isn't too disappointed when this oil deal doesn't materialize, or too devastated when Jeff leaves town.''

''Yes, that makes two of us.''

Lynn gave her cousin a sympathetic smile. ''We'll breeze the horses one lap around the track, then when we reach the quarter pole, we'll race flat out to the first turn, then cool them down the rest of that lap. Okay?''

''Be prepared to eat my dust,'' Beverly challenged.

''Ha!'' Lynn responded as both women urged their horses into an easy canter.

JEFF RAN HIS FINGER along a line that Hank had drawn on the map. ''Are you sure that's where the boundaries are? I don't want to be caught trespassing on someone else's property.''

''There's a little pond in one corner, the ruins of an old cabin in the other and a road runs across the front. Even if the fences are down, you oughta be able to figure out pretty close where the property lines run.''

''Hank, now don't take this wrong, but suppose you and I *both* believe there's oil there. How could we afford to drill? No big company's going to bankroll such a small project and under mere speculation. And I'll be honest with you. I barely have two nickels to rub together right now.''

''Don't worry about money, son. You find the oil, then we'll find the money.''

''Are you going to bring J.T. into this?''

''Hell, no. Sure, he'd loan or even give me the money. But he'd be doin' it to humor me, not 'cause he cares about the oil. And if there's one thing I hate, it's bein' patted on the head and told to go off and play, like I was a child.''

There was a knock at the door and Beverly stepped into the room without waiting for a response.

"Well, if it isn't the Hardy Boys, studying their treasure map," she commented. "So what are we looking for today? Gold? Indian artifacts?"

"Dammit, woman. Ain't you got anything better to do than to make my life miserable?" Hank growled. But the smile dancing around in his eyes told her he was as glad to see her as she was to see him.

Beverly reached into the pocket of her pink uniform and took out a small plastic bag of cookies. "Here, I brought you something to help harden your arteries," she said as she handed them to him.

Hank looked at the bag with suspicion. "Did you make them yourself?"

"Hardly. I haven't been allowed to bake cookies since I set the home economics kitchen on fire in the eighth grade."

"What happened—too much kerosene in the cookie dough?" Hank teased. He took out a cookie, examined it from all angles, then bit gingerly into it.

"You heard about that, huh? I thought it would give them a little more kick." Beverly grinned. "It did, too. I mean really, kerosene…Karo syrup…it was an easy mistake. Could have happened to anybody.''

''No, I think it could only happen to you,'' Hank said with a dry, hoarse chuckle.

''And I brought you some good news,'' Beverly added, drawing out the suspense. ''But after all those cracks about my cooking, I don't think I'll tell you.''

She gave him a saucy smile and turned toward the door. ''I guess you don't mind waiting until tomorrow afternoon to find out.'' She waved. ''See you around.''

Jeff looked from one stubborn person to the other, then quickly crossed the room to stand in front of the door and block Beverly's escape. ''If you don't tell us right now, I'm going to kidnap you and take you to Alvin with me.''

''Oh, God, no. Not Alvin!'' Beverly exclaimed in mock horror.

''Oh, yes.'' He leaned closer so that only Beverly could hear him. ''And I'll lock you in your hotel room and make wild, passionate love to you until you cry for mercy.''

''Was that a threat or a promise?'' She wasn't sure if it was his nearness or his words that caused the hot flash of desire to streak through her body.

''I don't make promises. That was a prophecy.'' Jeff's whisper was husky and provocative, stirring memories of all the kisses they'd shared in the past four days.

Each afternoon he'd dropped by the ranch and spent a few hours working on Hank's truck. He'd hammered out most of the dents and sanded off at least three layers of rust. He'd confided in Cal and enlisted his help in tinkering with the old engine to bring it back to life.

Beverly had always been able to think up an excuse to wander out there to watch and even to help Jeff when there was something she could do. They talked about everything, from their childhood to politics. But the one thing they both avoided, by silent but mutual consent, was any discussion of the future.

And somehow, no matter what the topic, they managed to end up in each other's arms, drawn together by some force that neither was strong enough to resist. And it rarely stopped with just kisses.

She wished she could regret their lovemaking. But just thinking about it brought a smile to her lips. It had been wonderful. It had been special. It had been absolutely natural, as if they'd been lovers for years.

And it was evident Jeff felt the same way. She often caught his gaze on her, and there was more than lust shining in his silver-blue eyes. He never looked at her that his expression didn't reflect his genuine affection and a certain amount of wistful longing, as if he knew there were promises she wanted to hear. But these were promises he couldn't keep, so he kept silent.

He'd never said it out loud. But Beverly had seen it in his eyes, felt it in the tender way he made love to her and the crushingly possessive hugs he gave her when he didn't want to let her go. She suspected Jeff, like herself, had never been in love before. It frightened, yet fascinated him.

She wanted to talk about it. She wanted to pour out her heart to him and confess her feelings to him. But she didn't. And he didn't. Whether it was pride or fear or reluctance to press the issue too far, she kept her words of love inside and hoped he could tell she loved him by her actions.

"Oh well, if I *have* to go with you, then I

guess I'll make the best of it,'' she responded in a slow, sexy drawl while her fingers slid down the row of buttons on his shirt and ended by hooking on the top of his waist-band.

A hot spark leapt into his eyes. ''You'll go with me?''

''If we can arrange it around my schedule here at the hospital and a modeling job I have at the end of next week, sure, I'll ride along with you.''

Oblivious to Hank, Jeff pulled Beverly into his arms and gave her a long, steamy kiss. By the time their lips parted, her knees were so weak, she was glad he kept his arm around her waist as he turned her toward Hank.

''Hey, did you hear that? Beverly's going with me.''

''If y'all are through smoochin' over there, maybe Beverly will tell me the news.''

''The news?'' Beverly echoed, all other thoughts driven from her mind by Jeff's embrace.

''Yes, dang it, girl. *The news* about me that you were so all-fired excited about.'' He straightened the top of the sheet and pretended nonchalance. "Not that I really care or anythin'. But you might as well tell me and get it out of your system."

"Oh, *that* news," she said, remembering what Glenda had told her earlier that afternoon. "Grandpa Hank, I hope you haven't gotten too used to being waited on and pampered...."

"Pampered, hell! They treat me worse than I treat a sick horse."

Beverly continued, ignoring his outburst. "You'd better pack your things because you're going home as soon as the doctor signs the release."

"Hot dang!" He tossed back the sheet and swung his legs over the side of the bed. But as he sat up, he began to sway.

"Whoa, slow down," Beverly said, rushing over to steady him until the dizzy spell passed. "You haven't completely recovered from that stroke, and you're still going to have to take it easy. Just because you've been walking around and you're getting to go home doesn't mean everything's back to normal yet. You're going to be weak and unsteady on your feet for quite a while, so don't push yourself."

"You sound like a doctor, missy," Hank said, accepting her help in getting out of the bed. "In fact, you've got a better bedside manner than those docs that have been pokin' and proddin' me like I was some sort of medical freak."

Jeff stepped closer and dropped a kiss on top of Beverly's golden head. "I've been trying to tell her she should think about becoming a real nurse…but you might have hit on an even better career."

"Yeah, right, like I could be a doctor," Beverly scoffed. "I'd have to go back to school, and really study. Then there's residency and internship and—"

"If you wanted it bad enough, you could do it," Jeff encouraged. "You're young, intelligent, motivated, compassionate—anything you want, you can have."

Beverly's expression sobered as she looked up at Jeff's beloved face. *"Anything?"* she whispered.

"Almost," he answered in a soft, slightly apologetic voice.

"I ASSUME you've thought about this." Carolyn sat on the edge of Beverly's bed and watched her daughter pack.

"Actually, Mama, I'm trying *not* to think about it. For the first time in my life I'm listening to my heart and not my head."

"You know I've always been supportive of you in everything you've chosen to do," Carolyn said thoughtfully.

"Uh-oh. I hate it when you start a discussion like that." Beverly took a bikini out of a drawer and put it in the suitcase next to a couple pair of shorts and some panties.

"No lectures, Beverly. You know that's not my style." She reached over and picked up a blouse Beverly had laid on the bed. As she talked, she folded it neatly and placed it in the suitcase. "I'm very proud of you. You haven't always made the choices I would have made. But then you and I are very different people."

"Are you saying you wouldn't go if you were me?"

"I have no idea what I'd do. Love has a peculiar way of throwing things all out of proportion. You do love him, don't you?"

"Against my better judgment...yes, Mama, I do."

"And how does he feel?"

"I think he cares for me, too...as much as he can."

Her mother was silent for a minute, then sighed. "I just don't want you to make a mistake, honey. I don't want you to get hurt."

"I think it's already too late for that." Beverly turned away so her mother wouldn't see the tears that always welled in her eyes when she thought of life without Jeff.

"How can you be so calm about all this? I've seen you more upset when a guy forgot to bring you a corsage."

"I'm not really calm. I've just accepted that this is the way it has to be."

"But Jeff doesn't *have* to leave town."

"There's nothing for him here."

"You're here. His brother's here. He could find work somewhere and settle down."

"But, don't you see, Mama? It would have to be his decision. I can't ask him to stay. I can't ask him to give up his dream."

Carolyn shook her head. "But what about *your* dreams?"

"What dreams? I don't have any. I thought I wanted to marry a rich, successful man. But now I realize that's not what it'll take for me to be happy. I thought I wanted to be Miss America. But what would that have gotten me but a rhinestone tiara and a year of traveling around the world, giving speeches and opening malls?''

She turned back to her mother and cried, ''Until I find out who *I* am and what *I* want out of life, I can't ask someone else to change their plans.'' Beverly straightened and took a deep, steadying breath.

''The one thing I do know is that it's time I grew up.''

CHAPTER ELEVEN

"HANK SURE DID WANT to come along with us." Jeff glanced over at Beverly as they drove east on Interstate 10. The air conditioner inside the truck's cab was on full blast, in an effort to combat the ninety plus temperature outside. But Beverly, as usual, looked cool and beautiful in khaki shorts and a peach-colored sleeveless blouse.

"His doctor would never have allowed it," Beverly stated positively.

"If his doctor was Dr. Sinclair, I'll bet he would have *insisted* Hank go."

Beverly unfastened her seat belt and moved to the center of the bench seat. She snuggled against Jeff's side and ran her hand along the top of his thigh. "Still worried about Dr. Sinclair, are we?" she teased.

As her hand brushed his thigh, he groaned. This constant state of arousal was something he was learning to live with around Beverly.

Her scent, her touch, the sweet sound of her voice, the music of her laughter, all kept his libido in high gear. No other woman had ever affected him as she did. No matter how often he saw her or kissed her or made love with her, he simply couldn't get enough. She was in his blood. And she was in his heart.

They stopped for lunch on the way and arrived in Alvin in midafternoon. They found a nice motel right off the interstate and Jeff parked his truck outside the registration office. Turning to Beverly, he captured her mouth in a long overdue kiss.

"One room or two?" he asked, his lips moving against hers.

"I suspect we need only one," she whispered back. "How can you fulfill your prophecy from across the hall?"

"Hmm…yes, the prophecy. Wild, passionate love, wasn't it?"

He felt her lips curve into a smile. "I'm counting on it."

"I'll be right back," he said, reluctantly pulling away and opening the door. He paused outside the truck for a minute, trying to catch his breath, and to will his body to relax and calm down so he wouldn't embarrass himself. His tight jeans did nothing to hide his condition. Finally, he gave up and pulled his shirt out of his waistband and hoped it would help cover him long enough to get them checked in. And once in their room, he and Beverly could ''fix'' the problem.

An hour later, Beverly was lying in the curve of his arm, idly running her fingertips in lazy circles on his chest.

''So when do you think you'll be finished with Hank's truck?'' she asked, her voice low and sleepy with the exhaustion of complete satisfaction.

''I'm not sure. But probably within the next couple of weeks,'' he answered.

Both knew they weren't talking about the vehicle, but about Jeff. Both knew it was inevitable. And both were very sorry this moment wouldn't last forever.

JEFF STOPPED his truck on the county road, and he and Beverly stared at the cluster of tract houses.

''Is this it?'' Beverly asked, glancing from the map to the neighborhood and back again.

''God, I hope not. Hank didn't say anything about these houses. But then, they don't look very old. They couldn't have been here when the map was made. As I interpret his map, this overgrown stretch of land next to the housing development is Hank's.''

''How many acres are there supposed to be?''

''About twenty-five.''

''Isn't that kind of pushing it for an oil well?''

''I've seen them drilled on as little as five, but usually they like to have at least fourteen or fifteen acres because of all the equipment.''

''I'll bet it's pretty noisy. How do you suppose the people in this neighborhood are going to react to having an oil well in their backyards?''

Jeff grimaced. ''I think they're going to be madder than hell. But, we've got to find out if there's oil here and make sure Hank owns the mineral rights before we stir that hornet's nest.''

''And how are you going to do that—find the oil, that is?''

Jeff gave Beverly a measuring look. ''This

might sound a little weird to you, but I can feel it.''

Beverly's expression was skeptical, but she didn't voice any doubts she might have had. ''So, I suppose we're going to have to get out and walk around.''

''I'm not too crazy about the idea of walking through that myself,'' Jeff admitted. ''It reminds me too much of my younger days when I had to fight off the snakes to build the roads to where they wanted to erect the derrick. However, *I've* got to do it, but not today. I'll come out early in the morning when it's cooler. You can sleep late, then I'll take you out for breakfast.''

''You want to do this alone?''

''Yes, if you don't mind.'' He gave her a crooked grin. ''Somehow I always have trouble concentrating when you're around, darlin'.''

She leaned over and gave him a long, deep kiss. ''You got yourself out of that one, fella. So what's on the agenda for this afternoon?''

''I thought we'd go to the Brazoria County courthouse and check their records.''

JEFF AND BEVERLY stood in the lobby of the courthouse and studied the directory of offices and services located there.

"Okay, so where do we start?" he asked.

"How about the tax records? Surely they would show if Hank's name is still on the property."

"Who said blondes were dumb?" Jeff teased.

"A brunette, no doubt," Beverly responded with a sassy grin.

They rode the elevator up to the correct floor, then joined a line of people waiting to speak to the clerks. When it was finally their turn, the clerk, whose name tag said he was Jerry, could barely take his eyes off Beverly long enough to acknowledge Jeff.

Jeff swallowed back a surge of possessiveness, and tried to keep his cool. "We have the legal description. Perhaps you could tell us the name of the owner."

Jerry tore his attention away from Beverly and wrote down the legal description, then seemed to take an eternity to call it up on his computer. Finally, he leaned back and announced, "It says here, a Henry Travis of Crystal Creek, Texas, is the owner of that property, and all taxes are paid up to date."

"Then where would we go to see a deed?" Beverly asked. "We need to check on the mineral rights."

"That would be down the hall in records." The clerk melted under the powerful wattage of Beverly's smile. "I'll call a friend of mine in that department and he'll have the book pulled for you by the time you get there."

"Thanks, Jerry." Beverly stood and held out her hand. "You've been very helpful."

"It was my pleasure," the young man gushed, holding her hand as if he were honored to touch her.

"His pleasure," Jeff grumbled when they were back in the hallway. "Am I going to have to get used to every guy fawning over you?"

"Jealous?" Beverly's blue eyes sparkled.

"Of that kid? Ha!" Jeff exclaimed, then caught her gaze on him. "Okay, yes, I am. Isn't that stupid?"

"Absolutely crazy," Beverly agreed. "But I love it."

They arrived at the records department, and true to Jerry's word, the book was open to the correct spot. The records clerk was just as eager to help. He made them copies of the

deed and an up-to-date map of the entire area
around Hank's land.

"Did you notice the way those guys were
looking at you?" Jeff muttered as they left
the courthouse.

Beverly stopped at the top of the steps and
slid her arms around his waist. "Jeff Harris,
unless you're blind *and* stupid, you should
have noticed by now that the only guy *I'm*
looking at is you. Besides, I've noticed quite
a few females trying to catch your attention,
and you don't see me foaming at the mouth
with jealousy." She stood on her tiptoes and
kissed him. "I just keep it hidden better than
you do."

Jeff chuckled. He hadn't even noticed any
women looking at him. That was a first. Usually, his radar was tuned in to the feminine
frequency. But somehow, Beverly had
shorted out his system.

They drove back to Alvin and had a lei-
surely dinner at a local steak house before
returning to their motel room.

The next morning, it was all Jeff could do
to force himself out of Beverly's arms and
into the Gulf Coast humidity. A few minutes
later, he was parked in front of Hank's land,

surveying the waist-high weeds. It didn't take him but a minute to decide to make a trail with his truck before attempting to walk through the thick growth.

He shifted into four-wheel drive. There was no driveway, so he angled the truck diagonally to cross the shallow ditch. The tires spun in the slick mud before catching and thrusting the vehicle forward.

Mosquitoes rose in gray clouds from the tall grass. Cottontails, disturbed from their hiding places, bounded away as Jeff tried to locate the pond or the cabin that Hank had mentioned.

He finally found a pile of burned logs and guessed it might have been the cabin, long ago destroyed by kids or transients. A little further investigation found an almost dry pond about four hundred yards across the back of the acreage.

Parking his truck in the middle of the property, he opened the door. For several minutes he sat, hesitating to take that first step.

What if he didn't feel anything? How would he break the news to Hank? Jeff suspected that the hope and planning for this project's success was one of the main things keeping the old man alive.

Even worse, what if he *thought* he felt something, and he was wrong? He couldn't forget that his past few jobs had come up dry. Of course, he still believed oil was down there, deeper than the crews had gone. But there was always the possibility that he could have been wrong.

Coming to check out Hank's land was more than just a favor to the old man. Jeff was testing himself, trying to regain his confidence in his own abilities. It had definitely been shaken during the past couple of years. He *needed* to be right about this one. If he wasn't, not only would his career be, for all practical purposes, over, but he would waste every penny the old man could raise, as well as breaking his heart.

Hesitantly, he stretched out his leg. First one booted foot touched the ground, then the other, and he straightened, standing tall in the middle of the prairie grass.

He felt it immediately. It was as if the compressed energy beneath the earth's surface sent up vibrations.

Just to make sure it wasn't the truck affecting his sensitivity, Jeff started walking. But even when he was dozens of yards away from the vehicle, he could still feel the oil. It was down there. He was sure of it. And, just as he felt the oil lying patiently in the bedrock, he could feel the stirrings of excitement within himself—a different kind of excitement than Beverly generated.

It was the thrill of the hunt, the mystery of discovery, the ecstasy of success. The feeling was almost as good as sex.

Jeff chuckled. He certainly couldn't say that to Beverly. Women—no, not just women, almost no one—would understand. Only another oilman would know how it felt.

He looked around the property, visualizing how it would look with its wooden platform and steel derrick stretching into the clear blue Texas sky. Lights would be strung all the way to the top and around the entire area, so the crews could work around the clock.

Jeff had no idea how deep they'd have to go. That wasn't one of the things he could "feel." Soundings would be made and core samples taken to determine the best location to drill. And with both his and Hank's intuition being so strong, Jeff knew they would stick to it until the oil was reached.

And there were plenty of obstacles to overcome. Getting the oil out of the ground was going to be a much more difficult process than it would have been several years ago. There were sure to be protests from the subdivision's residents, and this property was now within the city limits and would require all sorts of permits. There was also the cost factor. It wouldn't be cheap to put together an independent drilling operation.

A fresh attack of mosquitoes finally forced Jeff back to the truck. But for several minutes longer he sat and considered the possibilities. Could he be wrong? No, he was positive there was oil, so sure he was willing to invest his inheritance. If the well was successful, he'd be set for life. If it failed, he wouldn't be much worse off than he was now.

Sure, it was a gamble.

But it was his big chance. Not only would he be instrumental in fulfilling an old man's dream, but Jeff would earn the respect of his peers. And last, but certainly not least, with his share of the money the well would bring

in, as well as the renewed proof of his oil-
finding skill, he could sit back and wait for
the job offers to come his way. Maybe once
Beverly saw that he could be successful in
the oil business, she wouldn't object to becoming the wife of a wildcatter. Sure, they
would both have to do a little compromising,
with Beverly being willing to accept a new
life-style and Jeff being willing to curb his
wanderlust as much as possible. For the first
time since he'd met her, Jeff could see a
chance that he and Beverly just might be able
to make their relationship work on a more
permanent basis.

Buoyed by the thought, he hurried back to
the motel room and slipped into the room,
finding Beverly, just where he'd hoped, still
in bed.

"So, is it there?" she asked, covering a
lazy yawn. "What time is it?"

"Are you always so full of questions when
you wake up?"

Her smile was slow like a Southern drawl.
"The only question I should ask is why it's
taking you so long to kiss me."

He leaned over and let his tongue trace
around the full curves of her lips before cov-

ering her mouth with his. "And I regret every second I wasted," he whispered as he pulled away. "But yes, there's oil down there. I can't wait to tell Hank."

He kissed her again. "And to answer your other question, it's after nine. How about some breakfast, and don't tell me you don't eat it because I've seen you."

"Now that you mention it, I think I *am* hungry." She sat up, looked in the wall mirror and frowned at her tousled appearance.

"Don't change a thing," he told her, his voice soft and adoring.

"But I look like I just woke up."

One corner of his mouth lifted in a grin. "I know," he murmured as he kicked off his boots and crawled back into bed with her.

Quite a while later, they checked out of the motel, ate breakfast, then headed toward Galveston. It took them almost an hour to reach the island city.

"My parents used to bring me here almost every summer," Beverly recalled as they crossed the causeway from the mainland. "We stayed at a beautiful old hotel called the Galvez. Have you ever been there?"

"I've spent a lot of time in Galveston, but

never at the Galvez,'' Jeff answered. ''That was always a little above my means.''

''Where are we staying tonight?''

''Hey, I'm temporarily wealthy since I got my modeling check, so why not the Galvez?

JEFF DROPPED their suitcases on the dresser and joined her at the window that faced the Gulf. Wrapping his arms around her waist, he pulled her back against him and rested his chin on top of her head. ''I'm glad you came with me.''

''So am I.''

He groaned and turned her around so he could kiss her. ''I think we'd better leave now if we want to do any sight-seeing. I'm afraid I can't be responsible for my actions if we stay like this much longer.''

''Just wait until you see me in my bikini,'' she teased and stepped away.

They spent the day driving around the island, stopping to tour a tall ship that was in the harbor and several old historic mansions. After a wonderful fresh seafood dinner, they returned to their room to enjoy their view of the Gulf.

Outside the full moon was reflected on the

rolling surf, sending a shimmering streak of silver toward the beach. In the distance, lights twinkled from offshore oil rigs and ships that were navigating the Intracoastal Waterway.

"This is like a whole different world from Crystal Creek," Beverly said as she reached around and lifted her heavy hair off her neck. "That breeze feels wonderful…so cool and fresh."

"And humid."

Even though it was almost midnight, the traffic along the tall concrete and granite seawall was still heavy as teenagers drove as fast as they dared and shouted and honked at the cars they passed. There were quite a few pedestrians still out, some walking hand in hand along the top of the seawall and others sitting on its edge, swinging their legs as they looked out at the water.

"I'm glad I came with you," Beverly said, turning in Jeff's arms and looping hers around his neck.

"I'm glad you did, too." And for just a moment he thought how good it would be if no matter which hotel or which city or even

which state he was in, Beverly was always
with him. He wouldn't mind waking up to
her face every morning or lying down next
to her body every night.

CHAPTER TWELVE

"LET'S GET OUT of here," Jeff said, as they waited while a large family paraded into the water, following the father like a procession of ducks. "I know of a more private beach."

Even though they were several miles down the shore from the city of Galveston, the beach was packed with people. Some lay on towels, soaking in the sun's rays, while others had set up elaborate sun shades of tarps or blankets under which they sat on lawn chairs. The odors of grilled hamburgers and hot dogs mixed with that of countless buckets of fried chicken and the fresh fragrance of watermelon. Frisbees whizzed past Beverly and Jeff and small children screamed and laughed as they floated on blow-up toys or built sand castles just above the water line.

Beverly nodded her agreement. They returned to the truck and drove south. They crossed another bridge, leaving Galveston Island, but continued along a road that followed the beach. The farther they drove, the fewer houses there were. Finding a deserted section, Jeff turned onto a road that had been formed between the sand dunes.

Since they could drive directly onto the beach, Jeff parked the truck as close as he dared to the water's edge, backing it up so the tailgate faced the Gulf. He retrieved the towels they had brought from the hotel and spread them out on the sand.

Beverly took the suntan lotion from the glove compartment and handed it to him. After stepping out of her shorts and pulling off her T-shirt, she asked, ''Would you mind putting this on my back? I don't want to burn.''

Jeff's lips curved into that killer grin. ''It'd be my pleasure.''

Beverly sat on one of the towels and pulled her hair forward over her shoulder, holding it loosely in a ponytail. Jeff shook the bottle of lotion, then squirted some on his hand.

The thick liquid felt cool against her skin, and his fingers felt wonderful as they massaged her shoulders. She sighed as he spread the lotion, but her sigh turned to a moan when she felt his lips nibbling along the tender skin at the base of her neck. The tip of his tongue touched her earlobe, sending lightning bolts streaking through her. She turned her head, eagerly seeking those lips she loved to taste against her own.

His breath was hot as he opened his mouth, devouring hers with an insatiable hunger. No matter how many times they made love, the sparks still flew as soon as their gazes met or their hands brushed or their lips touched.

"Oh, Beverly, I can't believe what you do to me."

"Do to you!" she exclaimed in gentle dispute. "Just look how you affect me."

He rolled her onto her back and his hand slipped inside the cup of her bra and pulled one of her breasts free. "Let me see, darlin'." His tongue left a wet circle around her desire-hardened nipple. "And, oh, how I love it when you get aroused," he murmured, his lips moving against her soft skin. He drew her into his mouth and suckled her as his hand squeezed and stroked her other breast.

Beverly's fingers raked through his hair, holding his head to her. She could feel him pressing hard against her leg and she breathed a ragged sigh. "How deserted is this section of the beach?"

Two trucks full of teenagers with their radios on full blast barreled past, spinning out in the soft sand.

Jeff lifted his head and moved away. "Not *that* deserted, apparently," he said and reluctantly rearranged her top.

They stretched out in the sun, Beverly still lying on her back and Jeff rolling onto his stomach.

"Tomorrow we have to go back to Crystal Creek," she whispered, obviously as unenthusiastic about returning to the real world as he was.

"Yes, I guess we do. I've got to tell Hank the good news, then see about collecting my inheritance so we can get moving on the project."

"Then what?" Beverly turned her head and peered at him through the dark lenses of her sunglasses. "You're going to invest your inheritance in Grandpa Hank's folly?"

"Yes, I am."

"How much money are we talking about?

I don't know much about oil wells, but I *do* know they're expensive.''

''I'm going to invest all two hundred thousand dollars.''

Her mouth opened, then closed as she turned her head away.

''Beverly, I know you think I'm throwing my money away, but you've got to understand that this is a terrific opportunity. If we hit oil—and I'm sure we will—then I'll be able to write my own ticket. All those oil companies that wouldn't give me the time of day will be beating down my door. I'll be doing the kind of work I love. Plus, I'll be financially set, so I can offer you a future.''

She sat up and looked down at him. ''Thanks a lot, Jeff. You make it sound like all I want out of life is a rich husband. Has it ever occurred to you that I might just want to be with the man I love?''

Jeff turned over and sat up so he could face her. ''You've never made any bones about wanting a man who could give you a comfortable life.''

''Yes, but that was before I realized that love was more important.''

''But no one can live on love alone. I

wouldn't even think of discussing the possibility of a future with you until I was financially secure.''

''But I have some money, and my modeling contracts should provide a pretty good income for several more years,'' she offered.

''Your money is your money. It may be old-fashioned, but *I'm* going to be the provider in my family. You might think love is enough now. But someday I might look into your eyes and see regret and resentment for me not carrying my own weight. And I couldn't stand that.''

''Jeff, if you really felt that way, you wouldn't throw away your inheritance. It would make good seed money. We could live off the interest or the dividends. Or maybe you could even start a company of some kind.''

''I *am* making an investment,'' he repeated.

For a few seconds longer, Beverly's eyes searched his, looking for some promise, some sign that he was joking. In one breath he was telling her he wanted to provide security for her, and in the next he was throwing away all his money on an old man's dream. Apparently, all the things Scott had told her about Jeff's irresponsibility and inability to handle money were true. He was willing to risk a guaranteed future with her for the remote chance of striking it rich. And Jeff, of all people, should know the odds were against him.

Beverly couldn't help but believe that, if he cared enough for her, he would go for the sure thing. But then, he'd never made any pretense that Beverly was his first love *or* his last love. In fact, he'd never mentioned love at all.

It wouldn't take him long to finalize his plans with Hank, and then, probably in less than a week, he'd be gone.

A cold chill raced through Beverly, totally chasing away any remnant of passion. She crossed her arms over her chest and turned away, suddenly feeling more naked and vulnerable than she'd ever felt in her life.

''I think we'd better leave,'' she said, wishing the tears weren't so evident in her voice.

''Beverly, I...'' His words trailed off.

''Jeff, when it's time to go...it's time to go.''

She could feel his hand stroking her hair, tenderly, gently touching it as if he was trying to remember the texture and curl of every golden strand.

"Maybe someday…" he began again, but she shook her head.

"You don't make promises, remember?" she said. "And I'm not asking for any. I respect your honesty." Her bare shoulder lifted in a shrug. "I may not have always liked it, but I can't say you've ever lied to me or told me something just because you thought I wanted to hear it. Please don't start now."

The ride back to the hotel was silent. But it wasn't a tense silence, it was one heavy with melancholy.

"Do you want us to drive back to Crystal Creek tonight?" Jeff was the first to speak. He glanced at his watch. "If we get started right away, we can make it before midnight."

"If you don't mind, I'd like to do that," Beverly confirmed, not quite meeting his eyes.

And since he'd seen the glitter of unshed tears in her eyes when they left the beach, Jeff didn't want to look too closely anyway.

He'd always been a sucker for tears. And Beverly's were doubly painful for him to witness. He knew he'd hurt her. And yet he knew there was nothing he could do to change things. He had to do what he felt was right.

Oh sure, he could get down on his knees and apologize. He could tell her he loved her more than he'd ever thought it possible to love another person. He could beg her to wait for him...for God knew how long until he could give her the kind of life she deserved. Or he could buy a small business and settle down to the life of shopkeeper in Crystal Creek and be bored out of his mind.

But Jeff knew none of those options was viable. If he didn't find oil he would have nothing to offer Beverly *except* his love. If he didn't try for the oil on Hank's land, the old man would never forgive him, and Jeff himself would always wonder whether his instinct had been right.

No. There was only one way to accomplish all his goals, and that was to strike oil on Hank's land!

But for now, he had to keep silent. And hope. More than anything, he hoped she would be there when—he refused to even think if—the well came in.

They broke the journey only for a quick supper in a truck stop and to fill the gas tank. Beverly leaned against the passenger door and slept, or pretended to sleep, most of the way. Jeff tried to concentrate on the road. But the fragrance of her perfume filled the cab of the truck. And every once in a while he heard what sounded suspiciously like a muffled sniffle. Jeff reached forward and turned on the radio, scanning until he found a good country and western station. He knew he was being cowardly, but he couldn't stand to hear her cry.

As he'd predicted, it was eleven-thirty when he drove through the Circle T's elaborate gates and parked in front of the sprawling ranch house. Beverly opened the truck's door immediately. Jeff took her suitcase and overnight bag out of the back and carried them onto the porch, standing behind her as she fumbled with her keys, finally unlocking the front door.

All the lights were off except for a low-wattage lamp in the living room. Everyone had obviously already gone to bed. Normally, Jeff would have welcomed the opportunity to spend more time alone with Beverly. But tonight, she didn't even invite him in.

Instead, she took the suitcases from him, flashed him a shaky smile and said, "Thanks, Jeff. I…" Her voice faltered and she took a deep breath before continuing. "I suppose I'll be pretty busy the next few days…. I might even have to drive to San Antonio for a modeling job. So, I guess I'll just say goodbye now…and good luck. I hope you and Hank find that oil."

She leaned forward, obviously planning on pressing a platonic kiss on his cheek, but Jeff turned his head and met her mouth with his. Startled, she began to pull away, then sighed and returned his kiss with a sweet wistfulness that touched him more deeply than any passionate response ever could.

"Goodbye," she whispered, her words hot against his lips, then she was inside the house and the door had clicked shut in front of him.

"Goodbye, Beverly," he said softly, and with the safety of the heavy, soundproof door between them, he added, "I love you, darlin'."

THE NEXT MORNING Beverly barely took the time to say hello to her mother and tell her where she was going before packing her bags to leave town. At first she'd considered actually going to San Antonio, even though there weren't any modeling jobs planned as she'd told Jeff. All she wanted to do was get as far away from Jeff as she could, so that she couldn't go to him and either throw herself into his arms and beg him to reconsider or admit that she loved him and would wait an eternity for him. Either way, she would be setting herself up for humiliation. Whether he accepted her offer or granted her plea, it would be because she'd pushed him into a corner and he had no graceful way out.

As much as Beverly loved Jeff, she wanted him because he chose to include her in his life, not because she had forced her way in. And part of her knew he *had* to seize this chance to prove he could still find oil. Perhaps at some point he actually *would* come back for her. There was even a remote possibility that the well could hit. She didn't want to think what would become of Jeff if it didn't. But she had to get on with her life…a life *without* Jeff.

Carolyn must have sensed her daughter's dilemma because she wisely made no mention of Jeff, but did offer a little motherly advice. "Gregory Sinclair has called here a dozen times, asking about you," she told Beverly. "He's a very nice man, you know."

"I know, Mama. He's exactly the kind of man I thought I was looking for. But I've made a startling discovery during the past couple of weeks. You can't pick who you love. And I don't want a marriage without love."

Her mother frowned, concern written clearly on her face. "So, what are you going to do?"

"Right now or long term?"

"Right now for a start."

"I don't know. I just have to get out of town for a few days."

"Why don't you go the lake house?" Carolyn suggested. "I don't think anyone's using it. I'll give J.T. a call to make sure."

Beverly considered the idea for a couple of minutes before nodding. "That might be just what I need. But," she said, leveling a serious look at her mother, "don't tell *any-*

one where I am, okay? I need the time alone.''

Carolyn nodded. ''Sure, whatever you want.'' She reached out and covered Beverly's hand with her own. ''Baby, it's not the end of the world. I know it hurts now, and you'll never forget him. But in time someone else will come along. I'm sure there's the perfect man out there for you somewhere.''

''I know,'' Beverly agreed. ''But it doesn't make it any easier to get over him. I just know I need to get away so I can think more clearly.''

''I'll call J.T. while you finish packing.''

''Thanks, Mama. Just remember—''

''I won't tell *anyone*.''

WHEN BEVERLY ARRIVED at the lake house, she unloaded the car, changed into a bikini, then went out on the deck. She tried to get interested in a book, then tried to catch a nap in the sun. But her attention kept straying to the driveway. Would Jeff come? Would he somehow pry the information about her whereabouts from Carolyn? Or maybe he'd simply sense that she was here.

She finally dozed, not waking until the

shadows of evening covered the deck. Trying not to feel too disappointed, she went inside, showered and put together a salad for supper.

There was nothing interesting on television, so Beverly put a videotape movie into the VCR and tried to get interested in it, all the while waiting…waiting for her Prince Charming to come to his senses. At midnight she gave up and went to bed, telling herself that surely tomorrow he would arrive on her doorstep. She would try to be angry at him for waiting so long, but he would flash that sexy smile at her and her heart would melt.

But Jeff didn't come to the lake house the next day. Or the next night. Or the day after that. In fact, when Beverly finally broke down and called home to see if anyone had called her, she got the unhappy news that Jeff had already left Crystal Creek.

He was gone. And he wasn't coming for her.

Beverly slumped on the couch and felt her heart tighten painfully in her chest. The tears she'd been holding back for four days began spilling over, flooding down her cheeks.

That was the trouble with dreams. They never came true.

CHAPTER THIRTEEN

"HEY, STRANGER, it's good to have you back," Glenda called as Beverly stepped off the elevator.

A romance novel slid off the top of the pile in her arms and Beverly nudged it with her foot, sending it sliding through the open doorway toward the nurses' station. She dropped the pile of magazines and books onto the desk, then bent and picked up the one on the floor.

"And it's good to be back. When I signed up as a volunteer, I never would have believed I'd actually miss coming here."

"So, how was your vacation? You look tanned and rested."

"Well, I don't know how rested," Beverly admitted. "I got caught up on my reading, but I didn't get much sleep."

"That Jeff guy kept you awake nights?"

"You could say that—except he wasn't with me for the past week."

"I thought I'd heard he'd left town, but I assumed it was to be with you," Glenda commented.

"No, he wasn't with me." Beverly busied herself straightening the magazines, aware that her hair fell forward, effectively hiding the pain she knew would be reflected in her eyes. "He's moved on to a new job."

"But I thought—"

"So, what's going on today?" Beverly interrupted, anxious to change the subject. "Are there any special requests?"

"We've had quite a turnover in patients since you were here last." Glenda handed her a clipboard across the desk. "Here's a list of who's in which room and their condition. As usual, some are well enough to be entertained, but some are better off resting."

Beverly glanced down the list and recognized very few names. "How about Mrs. Goodwin? I don't see her listed here. Did she get to go home?"

Glenda looked up from the chart she'd been updating, a startled, then regretful expression on her face. "Oh, I thought you

knew. Mrs. Goodwin died five days ago.''
She reached into the desk drawer, brought
out an envelope and handed it to Beverly.
''She asked me to give you this. I'm so sorry,
Beverly. I know how close the two of you
were.''

Without even glancing at it, Beverly took
it and stuffed it into the pocket of her uniform.

She must have looked as stricken as she
felt because Glenda rushed to add, ''You
knew she was terminal. It was just a matter
of time.''

''I know…I guess I was hoping for a mir-
acle…or at least a little extra time.'' Beverly
felt her throat tighten. Mrs. Goodwin had had
her bad days, but usually she'd been sweet,
funny and undemanding. It had been a joy
spending time with her, reading her the romances she loved so much and listening
while she talked about her family. It was
more than losing a friend, it was like losing
a member of the family.

''Bev, you can't let the patients get to you
like this.'' Glenda's tone was sympathetic,
but the warning was clear. ''Some of them
are going to die. We've talked about this in

the volunteers' classes. If you're going to keep working here, it's something you to have to learn to accept.''

Beverly dropped the clipboard onto the desktop with a clatter. ''Then I'm not sure I can work here anymore.''

''Don't make any hasty decisions, Bev. This has been a shock. But the patients love you. They ask about you every day. You have a way with them, and I'd hate to see you give it up.''

''I can't stay today, Glenda. I'll think about it and give you a call.'' Beverly whirled around and headed toward the elevator. Just as she reached it, the doors whooshed open and before she could react, a small boy ran out and threw his arms around her legs. His body, while frail for a child his age, carried enough momentum to almost knock her to the ground.

''Miss Beverly, I'm so glad you're here,'' the boy said. ''I've really been missing you. Every time I come for a checkup, I come here to see you. But you've been gone.''

''Why hello, Jackie.'' Beverly smiled down at the little boy whose leukemia had so recently gone into remission. ''Have you been eating lots of cheeseburgers and chocolate shakes?''

His thin face beamed. "I sure have." He lowered his voice. "And thanks for sneaking those candy bars in to me when I was here.''

"I was glad to do it," she told him in a conspiratorial whisper and gave him a thumbs-up sign. "I heard you're doing great.''

He released her legs and took a step backward, swinging his arms wide. "See, I've gained ten pounds. And look..." He took off his Texas Rangers baseball cap and bent his head toward her. "Hair. I've got real hair. Isn't it cool?''

Beverly reached out and stroked the sprigs of hair that were struggling to grow. Seeing the children with bald heads from chemotherapy and eyes that looked several sizes too large for their gaunt faces had been one of the most startling things she'd had to adjust to when she first became a volunteer. And now as she looked at Jackie, who still looked as if a stiff wind would blow him away and whose wispy hair was barely noticeable against his shining scalp, she thought he was the most beautiful thing she'd ever seen.

Kneeling in front of the boy, she looked directly into his eyes. "You're going to have so many girls chasing you in school next year, you'll have to run really fast—that is, unless you *want* them to catch you and give you a big kiss."

Jackie shifted uncomfortably, but there was an intrigued expression on his face. "Really? Do you think so?"

"I certainly do. I know if I was a little girl, *I'd* be chasing you."

That comment brought a blush to his pale cheeks. "Heck, I wouldn't mind if *you* kissed me," he said.

Beverly leaned forward and pulled Jackie into her arms. She gave him a big hug, then kissed his forehead.

The elevator doors opened again and Jackie's mother walked out. "I figured you'd be here," she said, shaking her head with affectionate exasperation. To Beverly she added, "He was supposed to wait for me outside the doctor's office, but by the time Dr. Holland and I finished talking, Jackie was gone. It didn't take Sherlock Holmes to figure out where he might have gone."

Beverly stood, but Jackie slipped his hand

in hers and she squeezed it gently. "Jackie and I were having a little reunion."

"Well, I'm glad he finally caught you. He insists on looking for you every time we come here." She held out her hand toward Jackie. "We've got to get going, son. I've got a dozen errands to run, and we're stopping by Baskin-Robbins first thing."

Jackie reluctantly let go of Beverly's hand. "Will you be here next time I come in?"

She looked down into his pleading brown eyes, eyes that were much too serious for a child his age. "I'm not sure what my schedule will be, Jackie. But I'm sure we'll bump into each other every once in a while. Crystal Creek is a pretty small place, you know."

He seemed partially satisfied by her answer, but continued solemnly, "Okay, but you won't forget me, will you?"

"Of course, I'll *never* forget you, Jackie. You're my favorite little boy, remember?"

He flashed her a toothy grin and said, "And you're my favorite grown-up friend, Miss Beverly." He pulled his baseball cap back on and gave her a jaunty wave before following his mother into the elevator.

Beverly turned around to see that Glenda

had witnessed the whole incident. "Don't say it," Beverly cautioned.

"They love you," Glenda said, ignoring her friend's warning. "And you love them."

Beverly shook her head and punched the Down button with a little more force than absolutely necessary.

She stopped by a florist, then drove to the cemetery. It wasn't difficult to locate Mrs. Goodwin's grave because it was the only new one on the well manicured grounds.

Beverly walked across the thick, emerald green lawn and stopped in front of a pile of fresh dirt. The pungent odor of the moist soil filled her nostrils, competing with the fragrance of the flowers clutched in her fist. With barely restrained grief, she read the words chiseled on the granite headstone: *Charles Edward Goodwin, Beloved Husband and Father 1911–1984,* and next to that on the same large stone, *Mary Gladys Goodwin, Beloved Wife and Mother 1914–.* There obviously hadn't been time for the year of Mrs. Goodwin's death to be added.

Beverly gently placed the flowers at the foot of the new grave. There were far too few sprays of flowers scattered over the mound.

She noticed that on either side of the main headstone were two smaller ones. One that read *Mary Ellen Goodwin, The Angels Sent You, Then Took You Back Too Soon 1935–1942;* the other *Charles Edward Goodwin, Jr., Dear Son, We Miss You and Love You So Much 1937–1967.*

All the stories Mrs. Goodwin had told Beverly came flooding back. She thought of how little Mary Ellen had died of tuberculosis when she was only seven. And she remembered the old lady's pride in her precious son Charlie who had been a pilot in the Air Force, as well as her tears, even after all those years, when she told how Charlie's Phantom jet had been shot down in Vietnam and he'd come home in a flag-draped coffin.

Except for a few cousins and scattered distant relatives, the old lady had been all alone in the world.

"I'm sorry, Mrs. Goodwin...so sorry," Beverly sobbed. She knelt at the edge of the soft dirt, and the tears began to flow. She cried for Mrs. Goodwin's last lonely years and her pain. She cried for not being there to hold the sweet lady's hand as she died.

Beverly reached into her pocket for a tissue, but her fingers pulled out the envelope instead. She'd forgotten all about it until that moment. For several long moments, she stared at it, not sure she wanted to open it, but knowing Mrs. Goodwin obviously wanted her to or she wouldn't have gone to the trouble of leaving it for her.

Finally, she slid her finger under the flap and tore it open. A light breeze tugged at the stationery as she removed it and unfolded the single page.

Dear Beverly,
I don't think I'll be on this earth much longer, so I wanted to tell you how much I've appreciated all you've done for me these past few months. Your sweet smile and cheerful voice always brought sunshine into my darkest days. And when I bored you with my memories, you always were kind enough to pretend you were interested.

I think my daughter might have grown up to be just like you. Anyway, I'd like to think so. You've brought so much happiness into my empty old life. I hope you will continue to brighten other sick folks' lives and make their recoveries or their deaths easier by just being there.

I'm sorry I won't be able to hold on long enough to tell you this in person. But I feel so tired. Thank you, Beverly dear. You'll never know how much you helped me along this last, lonely path.

Please accept my locket as a token of my affection. It wouldn't mean anything to anyone else, but at least I know you'll know what it meant to me.

Goodbye and good night, dear friend,
Gladys Goodwin

Beverly turned the envelope upside down and caught the shiny gold oval-shaped locket and chain that slid out. She snapped open the tiny doors and smiled as she recognized the faded photos of Mary Ellen and Charlie that Gladys had shown her countless times before.

''Yes, Mrs. Goodwin, I'll cherish this always,'' Beverly said as she clutched it in her fist and held it to her chest. ''I wish I could have done more.''

A big black thundercloud rolled across the sun and sent out a blinding flash of lightning, followed a few seconds later by an ominous rumble. It hadn't rained for several days, but from the looks of the rapidly gathering clouds, quite a storm was in the works.

Beverly snapped the sides of the locket together and looped the chain around her neck. "Goodbye, Mrs. Goodwin. I'll take good care of your memories for you," she said before standing, dusting off her knees and heaving a heavy sigh as she walked back to her car.

BEVERLY STARED out the window of the plane at the cloud cover that still shrouded Texas, and wondered what it would take to lift her sagging spirits.

Actually, the phone call should have done it. A month ago she would have killed to get such a call. But the past few weeks had made her reexamine her goals. She was no longer sure a career in modeling was what she really wanted.

But when her agent had offered the deal with Belle Cosmetics, Beverly recognized it as her big break. How could she turn down such a plum opportunity when she still had no other, more worthwhile plans? At best, being the latest Belle Beauty would help her get bigger and better jobs should she decide to stay in modeling. At least, it would occupy some time and put money in her savings account while she was trying to decide what her next step should be.

She reached New Orleans in late afternoon and took a taxi to the Sheraton at the edge of the French Quarter, where the photographer, crew and ad agency representative were also staying.

The bellboy showed her to her room and opened the drapes, revealing a lovely view of the Mississippi River. Beverly handed him a tip, then walked to the window and looked out. In the growing dusk, a large paddleboat looked very festive with twinkling white lights along its rails and cabin roofs as it floated up the river.

It wasn't the Gulf. It didn't look anything like the view she and Jeff had had in Galveston. And yet it triggered memories. Happy smiles. Passionate embraces. And a tearful goodbye.

Jeff. Where was he now? Was he back in that motel in Alvin, surrounded by maps and lists? Was he in a conference with oil executives, trying to negotiate a deal to trade crew and equipment for a percentage of the well? Was he rounding up the crew and equipment on his own? Was he relaxing with a cold beer in a bar? Was he alone?

Her mind always veered off in that dangerous direction. Jeff wasn't the kind of man to be without a woman for long. He'd admitted he loved being around females. Even when there wasn't a romance involved, he felt comfortable talking and flirting with women.

The thought of Jeff with another woman brought a fresh grip of pain tightening her heart. But it was inevitable. And Beverly knew she had better get used to the idea or else push it completely from her mind.

Awash not so much in self-pity as in despair and loneliness, Beverly yanked the drapery cord and the curtains slapped together, shutting out the view of the river and any memories it might resurrect.

She flipped through the messages that had been waiting for her at the front desk. She was to meet the others in the lobby at five o'clock the next morning so her makeup and hair could be done before they all headed for

the site of the shoot at eight. She was delighted to find a hello from Mike, the photographer on the project. And there was a
fruit basket and a bottle of wine from the
Belle representative.

Beverly yawned. It had been a long day
and she had to look fresh very early the next
day. She changed into her gown and pulled
back the sheets. It seemed that she could
never get enough sleep anymore. No matter
how long she stayed in bed, she could barely
rouse enough energy to get up. Sometimes it
hardly seemed worth the effort.

She flipped off the light. Well, as Scarlett
O'Hara said, tomorrow would be another
day. Hopefully, it would be better than the
past few.

"BEVERLY, move a little to the left. We're
getting shadows from that big bush," Mike
called, studying her through the viewfinder
on his camera. "Yes, that's it. Perfect."

The camera began clicking as Beverly
smiled, posed, moved slightly, changed her
expression and generally ran through all the
motions she'd done countless times before.

The first day's shoot was at a beautiful antebellum mansion that looked as if it had been frozen in time.

And, as usual, that night Beverly fell into bed, exhausted. Modeling looked deceptively easy, but it was hard work sitting for hours while getting made up to look "natural," then standing in awkward poses, trying to look cool and cheerful in temperatures that would melt candles. But now she welcomed the extreme fatigue because it kept her from lying awake, thinking about things she'd rather not think about.

The next day, the location was Jackson Square in the French Quarter. Special permission had been obtained for Beverly to pose on the statue of General Andrew Jackson in the center of the park, sitting behind him on his horse. With St. Louis Cathedral in the background and a group of street musicians in the foreground, there was an interesting blend of new and old New Orleans.

It was another hundred-degree day, and Beverly sat limply on a park bench, barely touching her food during the lunch break.

"Hey, kid, why so down?" Mike asked, sitting beside her and balancing his plate on his lap. "I would've thought you'd be all smiles at getting this assignment."

"I'm smiling on the inside," she said with a weak attempt at an outward grin.

"Terrific. That'll really show up on film."

Beverly groaned. "Am I looking that bad? Are the photos—"

"They're fine." Mike hurried to calm her fears. "Actually, they're better than fine— they're great! You're beautiful, as usual."

A muffled scream pierced the air. Beverly turned around in time to see a young man pulling a bloody knife out of an elderly lady's stomach. Before anyone could move, he'd jerked her diamond rings off her fingers, grabbed her purse and fled, disappearing quickly into the crowd on the sidewalks that surrounded the Square.

"Oh, God! She's bleeding like crazy," one of the lighting technicians cried. "Someone call a doctor!"

Beverly didn't stop to think, but ran across the manicured grass to where the older woman lay. As she knelt next to her, Beverly pulled off the expensive designer scarf that had been loosely knotted around her neck.

"Don't try to move," she told the woman. "They're calling for an ambulance."

"He stabbed me," the woman gasped as she struggled to sit up, obviously teetering on the verge of shock. "Did you see that? He stole my rings…and my purse."

Beverly pressed the wadded-up scarf against the woman's wound with one hand and pushed against her shoulder, forcibly making her lie back down. "Don't worry about those things. You need to lie still now. Help will be here in just a few minutes."

"But—"

Beverly smiled gently, but didn't relax the pressure on either the wound or the woman's shoulder. "No buts. I've had first-aid training, and I know it's difficult, but you need to try to relax. My name's Beverly. What's yours?"

"Wanda. Wanda Anderson."

"Do you live around here?"

The old woman peered into Beverly's eyes and must have seen something that reassured her, because she actually did relax a little. "I'm from Miami. My husband and I are here on vacation. He's taking a nap and I thought I'd do a little shopping. He's going to be so upset I lost all my credit cards...."

"He's going to be so glad you're okay, he won't care about those silly old credit cards," Beverly said positively.

"Oh, you don't know my husband. He'll have a fit. He told me not to leave without him."

"Which hotel is he at?" Beverly looked up at Mike, who was standing beside her, and he interpreted her silent request. He pulled a piece of paper out of his pocket and a pen, then wrote down the name of the hotel Wanda mentioned and sprinted off. "My friend Mike will tell your husband, and I'm sure he'll meet you at the hospital."

Beverly kept the conversation going until she heard the wail of the siren as the ambulance approached. "See, they're almost here. It won't be long now."

The paramedics rushed through the gates, following the directions given by curious bystanders. As soon as one of them knelt down and reached for the scarf, Beverly started to move away.

"Don't leave me...please," Wanda begged.

Beverly looked up at one of the paramedics and he nodded before joining his partner in a quick examination of the wound. Then he jogged back to the ambulance to get a stretcher while the other paramedic started an IV in Wanda's arm.

She kept an ever-weakening grip on Beverly's hand as they lifted her onto the stretcher, pushed her through the crowd and loaded her into the back of the vehicle. "Thank you," the elderly woman whispered to Beverly just before she released her hand and they closed the doors.

"Will she be okay?" Beverly asked the man as he latched the door.

"I think so. You did a fine job," he said as he gave her a quick smile. "You probably saved her life." Then he jumped into the cab, turned on the siren and pulled back into the traffic on Decatur Street.

The crew crowded around Beverly, some staring at her in amazement and others pounding her on the back. She looked down at her blood-covered hand and noticed, for the first time, the stains that were splattered across her outfit.

Belle Cosmetics wouldn't be too happy

about that, Beverly knew. But suddenly she smiled. It was the first genuine smile to break through the unhappiness that had been hanging over her for the past week. She felt good, really good.

Her smile widened. For once, she had actually done something that made a difference.

CHAPTER FOURTEEN

JEFF LEANED FORWARD, resting his elbows on the bar as he nursed his fourth bottle of beer and stared moodily into the mirror that stretched across the back wall.

"Hey, cowboy. You new here?"

He'd seen the woman approach, so he wasn't really surprised when she spoke. But he took his time swiveling on his stool to face her.

"I've been in town a few days," he answered as he let his gaze boldly slide over her.

The black leather *bustier* pushed up her breasts until they were almost overflowing the lacy cups. The bodice was snug and short, leaving a couple inches of bare skin between its hem and the tight black miniskirt that barely covered her butt. Her long, shapely legs were bare and a pair of red leather boots covered her feet. A month ago, Jeff would have appreciated her beautiful figure, young, firm, voluptuous…but now…

Now, he longed for Beverly's body. How wonderful it had felt pressed again his. Her breasts were so soft and full and her skin as smooth as velvet. His hands ached to touch her again. But, he reminded himself sternly, he might never have the chance.

"Beverly." The word escaped in a husky sigh between his lips before he could stop it.

"Beverly? No, my name is Marla," the woman said, a flirtatious smile curving her lips. "What's yours?"

He blinked and his vision focused on the woman in front of him. "Jeff," he answered and patted the stool next to him. "Let me buy you a drink."

"Sure, I'll have a beer." She slid up on the bar stool and crossed her legs, causing the miniskirt to ride even higher on her thighs. She took the bottle the bartender put in front of her and tilted it to her lips. After taking a big swallow, her tongue circled her lips in an intentionally provocative gesture. "So, tell me, cowboy, how long will you be here?"

"Until I get rich," he muttered, "or die trying."

She frowned as if she was trying to decide if he was joking or not. "What do you do?"

"I gamble with other people's money." At her confused expression, he added, "Oil. I'm putting in a well south of town."

Her eyes brightened. "I just love men who know how to use their tools," she said with a suggestive glance at the front of his tight Levi's.

"How about a dance, Marla?" He slid off his stool and downed the last of his beer.

"I didn't think you'd ever ask." The leather skirt stuck to the vinyl bar stool cover, revealing a flash of black bikini panties as she took her time pulling down the hem to a semirespectable level.

Jeff noticed and was mildly surprised that the sight had absolutely no effect on him. Attributing this to one drink too many, he draped his arm around Marla's shoulders and led her to the dance floor. She melted against him, immediately looping her arms around his neck with the intimacy of a lover. A Garth Brooks song flowed from the jukebox. Jeff tried to ignore the words as he held

Marla much too close and tried to forget the woman he'd rather have in his arms. When Garth sang about being able to walk away from everyone except the one woman he loved, Jeff tightened his grip. As the song continued with Garth saying he'd never been in love like that before, Marla found Jeff's mouth and kissed him. Hard. Hungrily.

''What's the matter, cowboy? Don't I turn you on?'' she asked as he turned his head away.

He stepped back. For a long moment he stared at her, noting every beautiful curve of her body and wondering why she was having absolutely no effect on him. She was sexy, had a great figure, long blond hair, an attractive face. Normally, he would have responded to her immediately. Marla had everything he usually looked for in a woman.

But she wasn't Beverly. The components were the same, but the finished product was different. Marla didn't have Beverly's sassy sense of humor or Beverly's vulnerability or Beverly's surprising innocence. The truth of the matter was, no other woman would ever measure up to Beverly.

And as his thoughts again drifted to her, it

wasn't her physical perfection that made him ache for her. Instead, he smiled at memories of her charming the children with that silly dummy of hers and of the many hours she had spent with Hank and the other patients even after her shifts were over. He was impressed by her gentleness and patience regardless of the task she was given at the hospital. He doubted he could have lasted there more than a day.

The more he got to know Beverly, the more obvious it had become. Beneath that beautiful body was a heart as big as Texas, and Jeff's own chest tightened.

Garth had been right…Jeff was in love as he'd never been before, and Beverly was definitely the one woman from whom he couldn't walk away.

"Cowboy? Are you okay?"

Jeff's head snapped up. He'd forgotten about Marla.

"No, as a matter of fact, I'm not. I'm feeling a little sick," he told her. "Why don't I just take you home?"

"No thanks. I rode with a friend, and I'll head on back over there to meet her."

"I'm sorry," he muttered.

Marla snorted and tossed her mane of blond hair over her shoulder. Without another word, she marched across the room.

LYING ON HIS BACK with his hands behind his head on the pillow, Jeff stared at the ceiling and tried to think how he was going to get through the next fifty or sixty years without Beverly. Would this pain that was wringing all the life from his heart ever ease? Would he ever be able to say her name without his breath catching in his throat? When he heard the inevitable news that she'd met that perfect man and married him, would he ever be able to smile again?

God, what had she done to him? What spell had she cast? He couldn't even concentrate on negotiations for the well, which was extremely unusual for him. Oil had always dominated his life, his thoughts, his dreams. Now a sweet, exciting woman had become a permanent part of all those things.

Had they really been such a bad match? He remembered the happy lilt of her laughter and the sparkle in her eyes. He remembered the shaky moans that had shaken her body as she reached an orgasm beneath him. He remembered the fun they had had at the picnic, visiting Hank, meeting behind the barn to work on the old truck, and all the times they had gone for long walks to the horse pastures or the evenings they'd spent in each other's arms. Those certainly weren't the actions of a woman who didn't care for him.

She'd never told him she loved him. But she wasn't the type of woman to get so deeply involved with a man if her heart wasn't involved…at least a little. Surely all those emotions he'd sensed stirring within her hadn't been his imagination.

Of course, he'd never told her he loved her, either, and look how deep his feelings were. Several times, the words had been pushing against his lips, dying to burst out. However, he'd held back, knowing that once he actually said them, he'd be leaving himself wide open for her to break his heart. Somehow, as long as he kept his feelings to himself, he could protect himself from the pain and the humiliation. Once the words were spoken, he would be passing all control of the situation to her.

So what had he gained by keeping silent? Had he spared himself any pain? Was being in control of this misery such a prize? She still filled his heart, his mind, his soul. The only thing he had left was his pride.

And Jeff was discovering that pride made a very cold, lonely companion.

He glanced at the clock. It was almost two in the morning. Where was she? Whom was she with? The possibilities rumbled through his brain, increasing his pain rather than offering a respite.

He *had* to talk to her. How foolish he'd been to leave her without at least telling her how he felt. So what did he have to lose? Certainly not his heart. It was already lost forever. Certainly not a good night's sleep, because he hadn't had one of those since the last time she'd cuddled next to him and slept in his arms.

If he could just tell her how he felt, perhaps he'd be able to focus on his future. He needed to know whether or not that future included her.

That was it! He had to talk to her, face-to-face.

IT WAS JUST AFTER seven o'clock when Jeff drove into Crystal Creek. Fighting exhaustion, he stopped at the Longhorn, hoping a cup of coffee would revive him enough that he could talk to Beverly with at least some semblance of consciousness.

"Well, look who's back!" Dottie exclaimed as soon as he walked through the door. "You looking for Earl?"

Before Jeff could answer, Earl came out of the men's rest room and walked with a bowlegged swagger to the bar stools.

"Damn prostate ain't what it used to be," the older man grumbled. "I know where every bathroom in town is."

"Earl, isn't it a little early in the day for you to be out and about?" Jeff asked, sliding onto the stool next to the ranch foreman.

Earl looked surprised. "Early? Hell, the chickens have been up for hours, and I always get up before 'em. So, what're you doin' back in town? Got problems with the well?"

"No, everything's fine. I've applied for the permits, and I'm still working on lining up the crews and equipment."

Dottie put a cup of coffee in front of Jeff. "What can I get you for breakfast?"

He placed an order without glancing at the

menu. He wasn't really hungry, but he just wanted something to fill the time until he could go to Beverly.

"How does it look?" Earl asked, continuing their conversation.

"Great. I feel really good about this one. I'm hoping we have something going by the end of July."

Earl took a sip of his coffee, but his sharp eyes remained focused on Jeff. "Woman troubles?"

Jeff smiled. He doubted anything ever got by the old man. "Yeah, you might say that."

"Well, she's gone."

Jeff straightened, forgetting his fatigue. "Gone? Where?"

"I think I heard Val say New Orleans."

"Did she say why?"

"Something about being the new Belle model." Earl shrugged. "I wasn't *really* listening, but I remember hearin' she was stayin' at the Sheraton by the French Quarter."

"Damn!" Jeff muttered. He gulped the rest of his coffee, dropped some money on the counter and headed for the door.

"Ain't you gonna get some sleep first? You look like hell."

"Yeah, and I feel like it, too," Jeff admitted, dragging his fingers through his tousled hair. "But I won't feel any better until I see her. Talk to you later."

Jeff walked out the door and returned to his truck. After filling the dual gas tanks, he was on the road again, this time heading almost due east.

By the time he drove into New Orleans he was beat. He'd stopped only for lunch and arrived in the middle of rush hour. Inching through town in the heavy traffic, he finally reached the Sheraton.

"Can I get your bags, sir?" the bellboy asked when Jeff parked his truck out front.

"Don't have any." Jeff tossed the keys to the disapproving employee. "But you can get the valet to park my truck for me."

A glance in the mirror told Jeff why the bellboy had looked at him so oddly. A two-day growth of stubble darkened his cheeks and chin, and his hair was windblown and disheveled. His shirt was rumpled and his eyes bloodshot. All in all, Jeff knew he must look as if he'd spent a hard night on the town.

Oh, well, his mission was not to impress anyone except Beverly. What he needed right now was a room where he could take a shower, shave and generally get cleaned up. He signed in, picked up his key and headed for the gift shop to buy some essential grooming items.

But as he passed the bar area in the large, vaulted atrium, a flash of golden hair caught his attention. He stopped and took a step backward, wondering if his eyes were playing games with him.

Her hair, fashioned into soft, loose curls, was pulled up on top of her head. Her smooth, tanned shoulders were exposed by the strapless dark green gown she was wearing, and large diamond-and-emerald earrings sparkled on her earlobes. She was tilting her head back, laughing at something her companion was saying, and as Jeff watched, she leaned forward.

The man she was with closed the distance between them and kissed her on the cheek.

Jeff knew he should take that as his answer. Obviously, Beverly was a more skilled hunter than he'd given her credit for. She hadn't been in New Orleans but a few days and already she'd found a new boyfriend.

If he'd been thinking clearly, he would have just gone up to his room, got a good night's sleep, then headed back to Alvin the next morning.

Unfortunately, extreme exhaustion and a hint of a hangover from the night before rattled his judgment. Beverly was *his* woman, whether she knew it or not. How dared she go so quickly into the arms of another man when she already had a man who loved her to distraction!

Jeff stalked across the open reception area, not stopping until he stood in front of her.

"Jeff!" Beverly gasped. "What on earth are you doing here?"

"Let's go," he said, grabbing her by the wrist. "I want to talk to you."

Beverly glanced around at the people who had halted their conversations and were openly eavesdropping on hers. Spots of color darkened her cheeks. She looked back at Jeff. "What about?"

"I love you, Beverly. There, I've said it!" Jeff looked around the room and grinned sheepishly. "And I seem to have plenty of witnesses."

"Jeff—you've got more than live witnesses. You've now been filmed for posterity. I'm in the middle of a shoot here."

Way to go, Jeff. Make a complete idiot of yourself. How on earth did you miss the cameras and the lights? Of course, he knew how he'd missed seeing all the apparatus. He'd had eyes only for Beverly.

Beverly turned to the male model, who had placed his arm protectively over hers as Jeff had grabbed her. "Please excuse me." She moved into Jeff's waiting embrace. Neither noticed the round of applause that greeted their kiss. Only the popping of camera flashes finally drew them apart.

"Thank you, thank you." Jeff bowed playfully to the crowd. "It's been a pleasure, but we're leaving now."

"But..."

In a movement so quick it surprised them both, he leaned over and lifted her until she was lying bent over his shoulder.

"What are you doing?" she asked, clinging to him as he carried her across the lobby.

"We're going to finish this in my room."

He stopped at the elevator and pushed the button.

Once alone inside the elevator, Jeff let Beverly slide to the floor.

"That was an abrupt exit," she said, but her eyes were begging for a kiss, which he promptly gave her.

"I don't want to share you with anyone," he said when their lips separated again. "At least not for the next hundred years or so."

"That's going to be difficult in my line of work," she said.

"Your line of work?" he echoed. "You mean modeling?"

"No, I mean medicine. I've been thinking a lot about it the past few days, and I've decided to use one of my pageant scholarships to go to med school."

He smiled and kissed her again. "You'll be a wonderful nurse."

She laughed. "Oh no, I'm aiming higher than that. I'm going to become a doctor." Her hand lifted to the antique locket that hung around her neck. "Yes, I think it's something I can do well. And it's time I did something worthwhile."

"I can think of something else worthwhile you can do."

"Oh? What would that be?"

He pulled her back into his arms and gave her a warm, possessive hug. "You can tell me you love me."

"And how is that worthwhile?"

"If you do, you can take full credit for redeeming a scoundrel."

"What happened to all that 'listening to the wind' talk?" she asked, obviously still cautious. "I realize now the man who's perfect for me may not be rich, but I do expect him to be with me."

"When I compared listening to the wind against listening to my heart, I had to go with what my heart's saying." He looked deeply into her eyes, trying to convince her that his feelings were genuine. "Things might not always be easy for us, Beverly. But together we can make it. I can't be happy without you. I don't even want to try. You are my one true love."

All doubt melted from her eyes. "Is this a proposal?"

"It's a prophecy. I'll make you happy, and I'll love you forever."

"Then yes, Jeff darlin'. I love you and I'd be proud to become your wife."

The elevator doors opened as he leaned closer and captured her mouth in a long, loving kiss.

"Remember when I said there weren't any good men left?" Beverly whispered. "Now it's really true because I just got the last one."

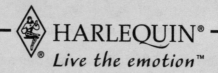

HARLEQUIN®
Live the emotion™

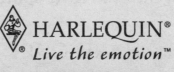

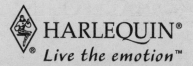

HARLEQUIN®
INTRIGUE®

BREATHTAKING ROMANTIC SUSPENSE

Shared dangers and passions lead to electrifying romance and heart-stopping suspense!

Every month, you'll meet six new heroes who are guaranteed to make your spine tingle and your pulse pound. With them you'll enter into the exciting world of Harlequin Intrigue— where your life is on the line and so is your heart!

THAT'S INTRIGUE— ROMANTIC SUSPENSE AT ITS BEST!

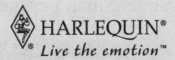

HARLEQUIN®
Live the emotion™

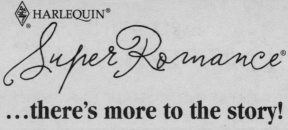
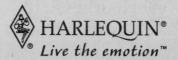